KU-213-454

sther Shaw was born in August of 1973, and has always lived in the West Midlands in the heart of the Black Country. She was always encouraged by her parents and teachers to broaden and express her rather extensive imagination.

Esther first started writing short stories as a hobby at the tender age of eleven. She was constantly told by family and friends that something should be done with them, but never took her writing seriously until one fateful night in the winter of 2002. After yet another nagging conversation on the telephone with her Aunty Janet, Esther promised she would dedicate her first book to her and she would see it in print within her lifetime. That very night, Janet's life was taken by a massive heart attack. It was an omen which motivated Esther to write *The Winter Mare*; the first instalment of a three-part story.

A lot of her time as an adult has been taken up with caring for the horses in the riding school where she works full time, and she has gained a lot of inspiration from the animals she works with.

THE WINTER MARE

THE WINTER MARE

Esther Shaw

ATHENA PRESS
LONDON

THE WINTER MARE
Copyright © Esther Shaw 2005

ISBN 1 84401 447 9

First Published 2005
ATHENA PRESS
Queen's House, 2 Holly Road
Twickenham TW1 4EG
United Kingdom

Printed for Athena Press

Acknowledgements

The author would like to thank the following people and organisations for their help in bringing this book into print:

Blackheath Library for allowing me extra time on their computers before I was able to acquire one for myself, and for showing genuine interest in my venture.

All the following people for their proofreading, input and suggestions: Auntie Aggie, Aunty Ivy, Kath, Angie, Barbara, Lillian, Jade; you all know who you are.

Thanks to Uncle Roy for the business advice.

A very special thank you to my mom, for putting up with the constant requests for inspiration; and for your encouragement in all that I do, both financial and emotional.

And finally, thank you to my late Aunty Jan and Uncle Don, to whom this book is dedicated. Without you I would never have had the inspiration to write this story and follow it through to print.

Contents

The Round-up

The Round-up

"It may snow today," predicted Dad as he placed Angel's breakfast in front of her. She took a deep breath, savouring the aroma of the smoky bacon, and smiled contentedly. Dad looked out of the window and up at the threatening yellowish-grey clouds. "It's early this year. Do you fancy helping me to bring the herd down today?"

"Sure," munched Angel.

"You can take the chance to see if there are any you fancy breaking in before we take them into town."

"Dad…" Angel gave a warning glare.

"Oh, come on! That old nag out in the barn has just about had it." He smiled secretly to himself. He loved winding her up like this. She fell for it every time.

"He's not a nag! He's fine!"

"It's a gruelling trip. He's getting on now, you know."

"I know how old he is! I raised him as a colt, remember?"

Dad laughed. "Relax, Buttercup. I'm only teasing."

"Dad! You know how I hate it when you call me that. I'm fifteen!"

"You're fourteen, and you'll always be my Buttercup." He laughed again at his daughter's tortured expression. "Eat your breakfast. We'd better hurry if we want to get them down before the weather changes."

"Yeah. Clare's coming round later. I promised we'd go riding."

"Have you not got homework to do?"

Angel cringed and avoided the question. "I'm going to get changed." She hastily scraped up the last few baked beans and ran upstairs.

"You'll get indigestion!" Dad called after her and sighed hopelessly.

There was already the hush of expectancy in the air that comes before a heavy snowfall as Angel jogged across the small yard towards the barn. Dad had already tacked up Ryan, the large chestnut gelding. "As quick as you can," he instructed as she ran past him.

Wirlwind nickered softly in greeting as Angel approached his stall. "Hello Wirlwind," she smiled, running her hand up to his neck to scratch his ears. "You're not a nag, are you? You're a handsome stallion!"

"Angel!" hollered Dad impatiently from outside.

She rolled her eyes defiantly. "Coming!"

The snow had already started to fall in large, floating flakes as Angel rode out to join her father and they set off towards the mountains at a trot. This had become a family tradition: every year, just before winter, they would head off and round up about fifty of their horses that roamed free for the rest of the year in their nine hundred acre ranch. On a good year they would sell for two hundred dollars a head in town, which provided them with a whole year's income. It wasn't much, but it was all they knew.

Finding the herd had never been easy. In places the land was rough with steep, rocky slopes. There were dense woodland areas and hidden meadows; and if the snows came early, the horses would instinctively head for higher ground, making it even more difficult. Even with Father's tracking experience, it took them over two hours to find them. The snow had fallen gently over those two hours and had formed a white blanket over everything. But at last they came in sight – about seventy-five of them – grazing peacefully. Then the dark bay stallion sensed their presence and squealed a warning to the rest of his herd. Before they could scatter into the nearby trees, Angel and her father raced to head them off, wheeled them around and began driving them towards home. Angel loved this part; thundering along with the snow stinging her face and the wind, bitter cold, making her fingers numb, even through her riding gloves. Soon they would reach the last stretch of open grassland. Here she urged Wirlwind on even faster to get ahead of the drumming mob, and swung open the gate to the corral just in time before the herd rumbled past and the gate clanged shut.

Then Angel noticed Clare's horse, Jake, tied up to the fence post, snorting restlessly at the exhausted herd, sensing their anxiety at being trapped. Angel skittishly searched the area and smiled as she saw Clare emerge from the barn. "Hi!" she shouted and waved.

"There you are," Clare replied and came running over to inspect the catch.

Angel jumped down to join her. This was the first time both Angel and her father had really seen the foals that had been born that spring.

"Not a bad round-up," commented Clare. "A few good-looking fillies in there, eh Mr Connor?"

"Yeah," he replied. "Tell your dad he's welcome to come over and pick a couple. I still owe him for that work he did for me a while back."

"Thanks, I'll tell him." Clare turned to Angel and smiled, playfully. "I've got something to tell ya!"

"What?" whispered Angel, enthralled.

"Hey!" called Dad as they headed off towards the house. They turned back. "What about that nag of yours? You're not just gonna leave him there are you?"

"But we're going out riding again later," Angel objected.

"At least loosen him up! Give him water! He's about to collapse!"

Angel sighed sulkily and took hold of Wirlwind's reins, leading him to the barn.

"Here! Take care of Ryan too!" Dad chuckled as she clomped over to him and reluctantly took Ryan's reins.

"Here, I'll take him for you," offered Clare.

"Thanks," replied Angel. "So what's this you gotta tell me?"

"Well, I've heard that Christine Baker is gonna be suspended!"

This was big news. Christine Baker was the school bully and she had made both Clare and Angel's lives a misery ever since they had started at Bloomsdale High.

Angel gasped. "Really? How come?"

"She knocked some kid's head against the wall and the kid's parents are suing!"

The two friends left the horses munching contentedly on some hay and walked briskly back to the house, chattering excitedly about the prospect of school without Christine Baker.

"Homework!" reminded Dad as they practically ran past him up to Angel's room.

"I can do it tomorrow," whispered Angel to Clare. She pulled off her riding boots and turned on her CD player before jumping on the bed and began brushing her long brown hair.

"Where shall we go this afternoon?" wondered Clare.

"I thought we could go over to Rose Point. It's not too steep down there."

Clare nodded in agreement. "Good idea. My dad said it's gonna be a bad winter this year. He's never wrong."

Angel grinned. "Maybe the school will close if it gets really bad."

"I wish!" retorted Clare, and they laughed.

As the day wore on, the snow became thicker and deeper. "We'd better go," observed Clare eventually, "or it'll be too deep, even for the horses."

"Yeah," agreed Angel, pulling her boots back on. They went riding every Saturday, and Angel always looked forward to it.

"Done your homework?" nagged Dad as they came downstairs.

"I'll do it later. We're going riding before it gets too deep. See ya, bye!" And they made a hasty retreat.

Dad just shook his head hopelessly. "That girl needs to learn some discipline," he said to himself and went back to his crossword.

In places, the snow was already knee-deep to the horses as they set off. At least it wasn't falling so thickly now. They hadn't gone far before Clare stopped, looking at something on the ground.

"What is it?" asked Angel, trotting to catch up.

"Are you sure you rounded up *all* the horses today?" asked Clare, puzzled.

"Positive, why?"

"There's tracks here. Fairly fresh too. They haven't been filled in."

Angel was just as puzzled.

"You must have missed one."

"No way," Angel insisted, and she began following the tracks into the trees.

"If the winter's gonna be as bad as my dad says it is, we'd better bring it in. It'll never survive."

"Come on. These tracks can't be more than half an hour old. It can't be that far away." Angel spurred Wirlwind into action, closely followed by Clare and Jake, and they cantered off along the track.

"Do you think one of them could have escaped the coral?" Clare wondered.

"Wait!" Angel skidded Wirlwind to an abrupt halt. "There," she pointed and frowned. Had she seen something moving in the trees up ahead?

"Where?"

Maybe she had imagined it. "Did you see anything then? In those trees?" Angel searched for some confirmation that she wasn't going mad. "I'm sure I saw something…" she stared intently.

"You're imagining things," concluded Clare suddenly.

But just then, there it was again – or was it a lump of snow falling off a bough, playing tricks with her eyes? Once again Angel led off, slower this time, and quieter. Clare followed silently. Just before they came to the edge of the trees, Angel froze. She held her breath as she scanned the snow-filled meadow and there she was; the most beautiful mare either of them had ever seen.

"Is she one of yours?" whispered Clare.

Angel shook her head and could only watch as the lily-white mare continued to dance gaily, kicking up her heels, sending the snow spraying into the air, then got down and rolled.

"Where did she come from?"

"I have no idea," replied Angel, "but I know where she's going!" And she dug her heels into Wirlwind's flanks and raced towards the mare at top speed.

As quick as a shaft of white lightning, the mare disappeared into the trees. Try as they did, they had no chance of catching up. And as the woodland became increasingly dense, so the snow on the ground became thinner until even the tracks disappeared. They searched and searched until they both began to doubt that they had even seen the mysterious horse.

"Oh, I'm going home!" Clare gave an exasperated sigh.

"Just a little longer." Angel was more determined. "We can't be that far off now. She's got to be here somewhere."

"There's been no signs for over an hour. She could be anywhere, and I'm hungry!" Clare turned Jake around and started back.

Angel sighed, and with one more quick glance around the surrounding trees, she too gave up.

"Are you gonna tell your dad?" asked Clare on the journey.

"Of course! He'll wanna know." If she was truthful, Angel couldn't wait to tell her father and hopefully get him to track and catch the mare. He was so much better at tracking than Angel was. He was bound to succeed where she had failed.

"I'll see you tomorrow," said Clare as the path forked into two.

"Yeah, see ya!" replied Angel, before heading for home at a hard gallop. They burst out of the final fringe of trees and tore across the meadow to the house. So intent was Angel on getting home to report to her father that she didn't see the pair of large, dark eyes watching her, hidden by the snow-covered ferns.

Poor Wirlwind was sweating and panting as they reached the gates to the yard. Dad saw them and came rushing outside.

"What's happened?" he frowned, concerned at the exhausted horse, every muscle in his legs trembling.

"Oh dad! You wouldn't believe what we saw. Come on, tack Ryan up. You gotta come and see!"

"You are goin' nowhere! Come on. Get down from there."

"But Dad! She was… beautiful. You gotta come!"

"Do as you're told!" he demanded. "Look what you've done to this poor horse!"

Angel jumped down and her father quickly untied the girth and slipped the saddle off Wirlwind's steaming back. "You gotta help me track her!" persisted Angel. "You've never seen such a beautiful horse in your life!"

"Here; you worry about this horse," he said as he handed the reins to Angel. "Go and get him cleaned up. Then we'll talk and you can tell me all about this 'beautiful horse'."

As Angel led Wirlwind back to the barn, her father looked curiously out over the landscape. Then he shivered and went back into the house. It wasn't long before Angel joined him, still just as excited, and proceeded to tell him everything she had seen on her ride that day. "It was definitely not one of ours," she concluded.

"Well, whosoever it is, it sounds like they're gonna want it back."

"So we're gonna catch it?" Angel grinned triumphantly.

"Maybe it broke through from the Dougals' place." Tom Dougal was Clare's father. "We should check the fences tomorrow."

"I think Clare would have recognised it if it was one of theirs," Angel pointed out. The last thing she wanted was to have to check nine hundred acres of fencing! It was a tedious job, which always took all day.

Dad smiled, knowingly. "Maybe you're right."

Angel gave a sigh of relief.

"I should still check the fences though; just to be sure." He laughed at the colour draining out of his daughter's face. "Don't worry. I think I can manage on my own. That nag of yours could do with a day's rest anyway."

Angel forced back the argument that she was meant to be going out riding with Clare again tomorrow, with the fear that she would get roped into helping her father instead. "Yeah," she agreed. "Besides, I've got homework to do."

Dad raised his eyebrows in surprise.

"What?"

"Nothin'! Its just I didn't know you hated checking fences that much. I mean, you'd rather be doing homework? Must be bad." He was winding her up again and she was embarrassed. He laughed. "You go and make us a coffee and then we can start going over the herd; see what we've got, OK?"

Angel smiled. That was a job she didn't mind doing.

So, after a brief break, they were back out in the cold. First of all they released about thirty of the good-looking mares, and, of course, Nugget, the breeding stallion, who was still in his prime, into the winter paddock. There they would spend the winter months being watered and fed on hay to keep them in pristine condition. Then, in late April, when the snow began receding, they would be released to roam the mountains and breed for another year. They seemed to accept that this paddock was the best place to be when the blizzards raged high up in the mountains. They had a large shelter at the far end and regular food and water, so never attempted to escape from the fairly flimsy, low confines of the paddock. Then came the part that Angel really enjoyed. The rest of the mares and foals had to be roped and given a general health check to make sure they were well enough to be sold. Dad dealt with the stronger and sometimes more dangerous fully grown mares, and Angel was left with the younger, and cuter, colts and fillies. There were, as Clare had said, some very fine-looking foals. It looked like this was going to be a good year. Tom came round later and claimed a couple of the best ones. He was officially a sheep breeder, but he knew a good horse when he saw one.

"Sure you don't want anything for these?" he asked.

"No! You take 'em," insisted Dad.

"Hey, Mr Dougal; have you lost one of your mares?" Angel piped up.

"No," he replied. "Clare mentioned you saw one today. Sounds like a good 'un. Maybe you should keep her. She might throw a few good foals."

"Yeah, maybe." Dad didn't sound too convinced.

"Oh, Mr Dougal!" called Angel as he began to ride off, leading his two fillies. "Would you tell Clare I can't come riding tomorrow? I've got homework."

"Sure. I'll tell her."

"Yeah, and tell her I'm having the doctor out to her tonight!" Dad laughed.

"*Not* funny!" retorted Angel, thumping his arm.

"You see this? Parent abuse!" Dad playfully ran off, with Angel close behind. They often goofed around like this. Angel always lost. This time she ended up with manure rubbed into her hair. Once again humiliated, yet rather happy, she headed off for a shower.

By the time she came out, Dad had finished off the rest of the sorting and was relaxing with a book in front of the blazing fire. Once he got his book out, Angel knew he was not going to move. Doesn't look like we're goin' trackin', she thought to herself, and decided to attempt to make a dent in the pile of homework. The amount of work they expected her to do over one weekend was ridiculous. How she hated school! Though she tried, there was no way she could get it all done in one evening. She worked well into the night.

On the way to bed, Dad noticed that Angel's light was still on and peeped into her room. She had fallen asleep at her desk. He smiled and gently picked her up and put her into bed. As she slept, he realised that she was becoming more and more like her mother. Even though it had been over thirteen years, he had never got over losing her. He stood for a while, looking out of the window. Sonia, his wife, had loved this place so much. She had said that she would never leave it, so maybe, in some ways, she was there with him. With that comforting thought, he went to bed.

Angel was woken the following morning at dawn by the unmistakable scream of Nugget, protesting at the fact that over half of his mares were out of his reach. Dad was preparing them to be taken into town. If she didn't hurry, he was liable to leave without her! She opened the window. "Dad!" she called. "Wait! I'm coming with you."

"You get your homework done," he called back. "I won't be long!" He opened the coral gate and drove them all out and off towards town.

"Damn!" Angel cursed.

Dad had always preferred to do business talk on his own. "The sales are no place for kids," he'd always say. But Angel loved the bustle of the horse sales and always tried to find some excuse to go. However, she had missed out this year. If it hadn't been for all that damned homework keeping her up half the night she would probably have been up earlier! Anyway, she wasn't prepared to start homework again this early in the day. She went downstairs to make herself some breakfast.

She was just finishing cleaning out Wirlwind's stall when Dad returned, leading two slender young mares that he had bought for the bargain price of a hundred and fifty dollars for the pair.

"What do you think?" he asked, allowing them to stretch their quivering noses over the paddock fence curiously towards Nugget.

"Nice," she replied, patting Ryan's neck as Dad jumped out of the saddle. "But I wanted to come!"

Dad smirked mischievously. "I was talking to Nugget! And you know the sales—"

"I'm not a kid any more!" Angel interrupted. "I'm gonna have to learn the business side of things sometime, you know."

"I know," smiled Dad. "And you will; when you're old enough."

"Why do all parents talk like that?" she said sulkily.

"It's the way adults talk. When you understand that, then you can start learning the business. Now, am I gonna get a drink or what?"

"You will," she laughed, "when you're old enough!"

He took a playful swipe at her as she ran off back to the house.

Dad decided not to let the new mares loose in the paddock. He liked to be around when he did the first introductions in case there was any trouble with the rest of the herd accepting them. He had a busy day fence checking, so he set them up with a stall in the barn until he had more time. He didn't bother to untack Ryan; just gave him a net of hay to chew on while he had his drink.

Angel had already filled his flask and was just wrapping up some sandwiches for him.

Dad smiled. "What would I do without you?"

"Starve, probably," quipped Angel.

He quickly gulped down his coffee. "Right," he announced, grabbing his saddlebag, "I'm off. You make sure you get that homework done."

"I will!" Angel rolled her eyes.

"Good girl. I'll see you later."

She watched him trot off into the distance until he was out of sight, and then sighed. She still had a load of history and maths homework to do before tomorrow, so she set off up to her room, where she spent most of the day. She would have been finished a lot sooner had it not been for the fact that she was daydreaming for most of the time; about the white mare. She imagined herself riding her across crisp, unbroken snow. Then something broke her out of her daydream. She stared out of the window and saw again the spray of snow. Could it be...? Yes! Just visible over the rim of the hill, far in the distance; Angel was sure it was the mare. She watched just long enough to see her gallop across the face of the hill before rushing downstairs and outside. The mare had gone, but Angel was not put off so easily. She looked at her watch – half past three. She would be back before her father returned.

Wirlwind snorted, startled when Angel burst into the barn. "It's OK," she reassured him, her voice quivering with excitement as she slipped his bridle on. "Let's go for a ride."

She led him outside, not bothering with the saddle, and vaulted up onto his back and they set off towards the hill. She soon picked up the tracks and set off in pursuit, silently this time. It was not long until the mare came into sight up ahead. Angel followed, inconspicuously. Despite her best efforts Angel was sure she must have been seen a number of times, but the mare never bolted; but neither did she stop to graze. It was as if she knew she was being followed and wanted to lead Angel somewhere. Angel quickly dismissed the thought as ridiculous.

The mare led her into a valley, which Angel had never seen before – mainly because there was not one blade of grass here for the herd, just rocks, extremely dangerous, slippery rocks; and a number of dark caves. With a casual glance back, as if to make sure Angel was still following, the mare disappeared into the darkness of one of the caves.

After a cautious pause, Angel dismounted and followed. The cave was spooky, but there was still enough light to just about see the tantalising hoofprints in the mud, leading further into the cave. Angel looked back to make sure Wirlwind was staying where she had left him. He was staring at her, as enthralled and curious as she was, so she proceeded to follow the tracks until she bumped into the wall at the back of the cave. Angel frowned and bent down, not believing her eyes. The tracks indicated that the mare had walked *through* the wall! "That's impossible!" she whispered to herself, looking around. But sure enough, the mare had disappeared.

School

School

I t was getting dark by the time Angel returned home. The expedition had taken longer than she had anticipated. Still totally baffled by the mare's strange disappearance, she didn't notice her father waiting for her at the gate.

"Where the hell have you been?" he scolded.

"You wouldn't believe me if I told you." Angel jumped down and led Wirlwind back to his stall.

"How many times have I told you not to go wandering off on your own?" Dad followed her. "Answer me!"

"I saw the mare again," she confessed. "I followed her. It was really weird, Dad."

He frowned. "How come this mare only shows up when I'm not around, eh?"

"Fine! Don't believe me. I don't care."

"Angel!" called Dad as she walked back to the house. He ran to catch her up and grabbed her arm, forcing her to face him. "What's got into you? I've never known you to act like this before. What happened today? The truth!"

"I told you the truth! I followed her into this cave."

"Cave?"

"Yeah. And she just... disappeared. It was as if she just walked through the wall." She sighed. "I knew you wouldn't believe me."

Dad grabbed her arm again as she went to walk off. "I believe you," he said softly. "Angel, look at me. You're not to go there again. Ever. Do you understand?"

Angel frowned at the desperation in his face. "Why?"

"Just promise me." He paused. "It's just too dangerous. One false step and you could break a leg, or worse!"

"Is that where Mom... had her accident?" she guessed.

Dad pulled her close to him, pressing her head onto his shoulder. "I just don't want to lose you. Promise me."

"OK, I promise."

"Good." He smiled and let her go. "Now let's get inside before we freeze to death!"

★

Angel went to bed early that night and dreamt of her mother, whom she barely remembered. She had been almost two years old when her mother was tragically killed in a riding accident. All Angel could remember was the song she used to sing to her at night: "Scarlet Ribbons". She had one photograph of her, but no memory of what she looked like. However, the closeness she shared with her father more than made up for the loss. Life was good.

Well, it would be if not for Monday mornings! The start of another gruelling school week. As usual, Angel met up with Clare at the end of the path that linked their two ranches and made the short walk into town.

"Well, looky here! It's Dougal and Florence, the two cowgirls! Yee-haa!" jeered the all too familiar voice of Christine Baker as they reached the school gates.

Angel and Clare looked at each other. "Here we go again," sang Angel under her breath.

Christine came sauntering over with a couple of her "friends" and grabbed Clare's bag.

"Give it back!" Claire demanded.

"How's ya donkey?" she sneered at Angel. "Is it dead yet?" She tipped Clare's bag upside down and shook all the books out, saying, "Got any cash in here?"

Clare immediately bent down to pick the books out of the slush.

"Hey! Who said you could pick them up?" Christine kicked the books along the floor, splashing Clare's face with the dirty snow. She burst out laughing as Clare stood up, spluttering.

Angel could feel the anger in the pit of her stomach. "Shouldn't you be preparing for court?" she asked, unable to stay silent any longer. "You may want to change."

Christine pushed her up against the gates and stood right up to her, staring threateningly. "What did you say, Connor?"

"You're ugly, not deaf."

"Angel, leave it," advised Clare, just as the bell rang to indicate the beginning of school.

35

"After school, Connor, you're dead!"

"We'll see!" Angel frowned with annoyance as her stomach churned.

"Are you mad?" exclaimed Clare when Christine and her friends had moved off. "You just picked a fight with Christine Baker, the hardest girl in the whole school!"

"Maybe she'll learn a lesson or two!" retorted Angel bravely.

"Well, someone will sure get taught!"

"Thanks for the vote of confidence!" Angel stormed off, sulkily.

"Hey, Angel, wait up! I'm sorry!" Clare ran after her.

But Angel knew she was right. She was mad! She was going to get beaten to a pulp!

All through that day, Angel couldn't concentrate on her lessons. How was she going to get out of this alive, without looking like a coward? Yet someone needed to stand up to Christine Baker. Even her friends were only friends because they were scared not to be.

All too soon, the bell rang at the end of school, a sound which Angel usually greeted with a sense of relief, but today it made her practically nauseous.

"Maybe we could hide in the loos 'til she's gone," suggested Clare, sensing her friend's anguish.

Angel sighed. "No. If we miss her today, she'll still be here tomorrow. You should carry on home. You don't have to get involved."

"No way! It's 'cause of me you're in this mess. The least I can do is stand by you."

Angel smiled thankfully. "Yeah, someone'll have to mop up all the blood!" She forced out a laugh, but the

36

look of dread on Clare's face told her that the gag was not appreciated. As soon as they set foot outside they saw Christine with her gang waiting at the gates. Angel was still desperately searching for a way out of this, yet trying to look brave as they approached. Once more, Christine soon had her with her back to the gates.

"Someone remind me what this little bitch said," she prompted the rest of the gang. "Ah yes! Something about going to court. The thing this demented little horsey woman seems to forget is the reason! Some little brat opened their mouth to insult me and got their head smashed in." She grabbed Angel's hair. "So what do you do? Exactly the same, that's what. Now you tell me, was that stupid, or was that just downright dumb?"

"Aaow!" cringed Angel as Christine tightened her grip.

"So what is the obvious thing I should do?"

"Apologise," suggested Clare.

"What did you say?" exclaimed Christine, not believing her ears and feeling somewhat at a loss. Not wanting to let go of Angel's hair, she was unable to reach this insolent child with a death wish.

"I was talking to Angel."

"Oh. Well, I suppose that would be a start." She pulled on Angel's hair again, twisting her head round. "Well?"

"Sorry," whimpered Angel.

"What?"

"I'm sorry!" she shouted.

Christine loosened her hair. "That's more like it."

Angel, angry and humiliated, wiped her tears on the sleeve of her coat.

"Hey!" Christine grabbed her bag, pulling Angel back as she began to walk away. "Who told you you could go?"

"I apologised, didn't I?" Angel pointed out defiantly.

"You watch your tone! I said that was a *start!*"

Angel sighed, not knowing how much more of this she could take.

"You'll bring a hundred dollars to school tomorrow."

"A hundred dollars!" screeched Angel.

"Shut up, or I'll make it two hundred."

"How am I gonna get a hundred dollars?"

"I don't care how you get it. I saw your dad around here yesterday, trying to look like John Wayne. It was pathetic! He made a bundle with that bunch of clapped out nags. You can afford it." She laughed at the fearful face of her victim. "Now get lost, you pair of losers!" she jeered.

Angel walked briskly off, followed by Clare, but suddenly found herself being shoved forwards.

Christine laughed again as she and her friends jogged past. "See you tomorrow, cowgirls!" she shouted over her shoulder.

"Are you OK?" asked Clare, assisting Angel back to her feet.

The skin had been ripped off both of her knees. "I'm fine!" Angel snapped, snatching her arm back. "Not that you care!" And she limped off.

Clare frowned, hurt. "Well, excuse me for saving your life!" she called after her.

Angel didn't stop or look back. She felt terribly let down. Yet, had she really expected Clare to fight for her and get a beating too? Tears of pain and frustration streamed down her face as she tried to ignore her stinging, throbbing knees and get home as quickly as possible.

★

Dad had just finished fitting the storm shutters when Angel arrived home. She hadn't noticed the telltale roar of the strong north wind lashing the trees, bringing with it sharp needles of snow. Angel sighed; this probably meant she was not going to be allowed to go riding tonight and she desperately needed to clear her head! She also knew what was going to happen when Dad saw her. He could get so overprotective. All she wanted was to be left alone to feel sorry for herself.

"Dad, I'm fine!" she insisted with an exasperated sigh.

"We'll see." He practically carried her indoors. "Now, are you going to tell me how this happened?" he persisted, sitting her down in the kitchen and getting out the first aid kit.

"I fell over. That's all."

"Right. That's all. Just fell over?" It was obvious he wasn't buying that. "Who was it who pushed you over?"

Angel kept her mouth tightly closed.

"Right, I'm going up to the school tomorrow. Get this sorted out."

"No!" she blurted desperately. "I mean, no," she said more calmly.

"Well, this can't go on."

"I know, but it's my problem, OK? Honestly, Dad. I know you mean well, but you'd just make things worse."

He studied her suspiciously.

Angel smiled, trying hard to make it look genuine. "I can deal with it."

"You're so much like your mother, it's frightening!" He smiled. "OK. If that's what you want."

"It is." Angel smiled back and glanced out of the windows, hearing the wind already rattling the shutters. "It looks like it might be a bad storm."

Dad realised she wanted to change the subject. "Yeah. It's been warning on the radio all day. The horses have been jumpy too, and that's a sure sign of bad weather."

He wasn't wrong either! But he was never wrong. He was more tuned into the weather than the horses were; it was a gift. The storm raged on well into the night, uprooting trees and fences and testing their defences to breaking point.

At two in the morning, both Angel and her father were woken up by the sudden silence as the storm passed as suddenly as it had arrived. During the eight hours that it had battered and lashed the landscape it had dumped almost twelve inches of snow, and as the skies cleared, the temperatures plummeted and froze everything solid.

Angel flung open the curtains the following morning to be greeted by a Christmas card scene and smiled with relief. She ran downstairs and switched on the radio. Sure enough, due to severe weather, all schools were closed. Maybe, if her luck held out, Christine would forget about her tax collecting!

Clare rang later that morning. "Hi. It's me."

"Hello," Angel replied, not too friendly. She had still not forgiven Clare for her apparent defection to Christine's gang.

"How's your knees?"

"Fine."

"Oh... good." Clare sensed Angel's tone, but still attempted to be civil. "School's closed today."

"I know."

"Oh. OK. Do you fancy coming riding today?"

"No."

Clare paused. "Why not?"

"I just don't want to."

"Oh. OK," Claire repeated uncomfortably. "I'll... see you some other time then?"

"Maybe."

"Right. Bye, then."

"Bye." Angel put the phone down and noticed Dad's curious expression. She rolled her eyes. "I'm going to listen to some music," she said, and headed off back upstairs. Before she got to her room, the phone rang again. Angel sat discreetly on the stairs to listen.

"...I have no idea what's got into her," said Dad, and then he paused. "Oh, I see... I'll have a word with her. Tell her not to worry... Well, that's understandable. There must just be some misunderstanding. I'll see what I can do... Yeah, well that's what I thought, but she doesn't want me to do that. She told me that much… I know! They've been mates for such a long time!… Yeah, OK. We'll work something out… Oh! How are those fillies holdin' up?… Excellent! Great! Well, I'll be in touch then. OK, see ya, bye."

Dad heard Angel run quickly up to her room and took a deep breath in preparation. It was times like these when he really missed Sonia. She had always been the talker. He was more of a doer. But it was clear that Angel was in danger of losing the best friend she'd ever had, or was ever likely to have, and she needed a friend. So it was up to him to put it right. Would he ever get the hang of this parenting?

"Angel?" he called, softly knocking on the door.

"I don't want to talk about it!" she warned.

"Can I just come in?"

Angel sighed and relented. "If you want to."

Dad sat on the bed next to her. "That was Tom Dougal on the phone."

"I said I don't want to talk about it!"

"Fine. Don't talk, just listen. Clare's really upset…"

"Good!" she interrupted bitterly.

Dad frowned. "I don't understand. What's happened between you two?"

Angel just glared at him.

"Come on, Angel. We used to be able to talk about anything." He paused, waiting for a reply, but didn't get one so continued: "Clare says you think she doesn't care about you."

Angel scoffed and turned to look out of the window.

"If she didn't care, she wouldn't bother calling. She wouldn't be this upset. Neither would you." He stood up. "Think about it," he concluded before leaving her alone.

Angel sat in her room for over an hour, thinking over what her father had said. Even though Clare was obviously desperate to make up, Angel was too proud and embarrassed to bring herself to take the first step and call her. The tears of frustration welled up in her eyes again. Why was her life so complicated? She suddenly found herself pulling on her riding boots. "I'm just gonna take Wirlwind out!" she called to Dad, grabbing her jacket.

"Hey, wait a minute! I'm not happy about you going out riding today, not on your own. It's treacherous out there," Dad objected.

"Don't worry. I'll be careful!" she called, without stopping, and ploughed her way across the yard.

Wirlwind greeted her as usual, but stood fast as she attempted to lead him out.

"Come on, Wirlwind. Don't be lazy!" Angel laughed, as he pawed at the shavings on the floor, nickering softly. "You're getting too used to your home comforts. Come on!"

He submitted, and allowed her to lead him out into the crisp, but freezing air.

As Angel set off, she had no idea where she was going. It was as if she was on autopilot. Wirlwind was exceptionally nervous. The slightest sound would startle him, so Angel didn't ask him to go any faster than a walk. She knew there were patches of ice hidden under the snow and he was being instinctively careful.

Just as she was beginning to think about turning back, Angel realised why she had come this way; she had been drawn there – the place which had taken her mother away so tragically all those years ago. It did cross her mind that her father had forbidden her from returning here, but she dismissed it just as quickly. She knew the dangers and, if she was careful, there shouldn't be a problem. However, Wirlwind stopped when they reached the top of the rocky slope leading down to the cave. "Come on!" Angel nudged him harder, but he flatly refused and stepped back, throwing his head up into the air. "Oh, for heaven's sake!" she sighed and jumped down. "What is wrong with you today?" She tried to lead him down on foot, but once again he refused and continued to walk backwards with his head in the air, his ears flickering nervously. Angel frowned with annoyance. "What's got into you? Fine!" She tied the reins around the stump of a tree. "You wait here."

He snorted, pawing at the snow as Angel returned to the top of the slope. She just wanted to take another look inside that cave. She carefully stepped down onto the first snow-covered rock. "Stupid horse!" she mumbled to herself.

But Wirlwind could sense another storm approaching and stamped around, restlessly biting at the reins.

Suddenly, a single gust of wind nearly blew Angel off her feet and with a loud creak and a swish, a nearby tree was uprooted. Luckily it fell in the opposite direction to where Wirlwind was tied, but it still sent him into a frenzy and he reared up, neighing with fright. Feeling the leather reins restrict him he panicked even more, writhing and straining, desperate to get away.

Angel scrambled back up the slope to try and calm him down, but it was as if he was caught in a whirlwind himself. The reins snapped and he was away!

"Wirlwind! Come back!" yelled Angel, but to no avail. He was gone. A dark dread gripped her. How was she going to get home? And with another gust of wind she knew there was no point trying to walk back, not with another storm chasing her. The only thing was to find shelter and sit it out.

Angel reached the cave just as the first biting flakes of snow arrived. She sat, shivering and hugging her knees, praying this wasn't another eight-hour storm. Maybe when Wirlwind got home, Dad would come out looking for her. He would be so mad with her if he found her here. He was unlikely to come before the storm subsided. Maybe when the worst of the storm was over, she should start walking back. Then at least she may be spared the 'I told you sos' and avoid the lecture, possible grounding, and the ban from ever going out on her own again! She shivered again, suddenly becoming aware that her back was wet. She stood up and noticed the once bone dry wall of the cave had begun seeping water. She backed off into a dark corner and stared in disbelief as the whole wall began to liquefy, and cautiously out stepped the mare.

Angel held her breath as the mare stood for a while, contemplating whether to go out into the storm, before becoming aware of eyes watching her. "Easy," whispered Angel calmingly, stepping out of the shadows. "Easy now, girl. Don't be afraid." Her heart was thumping unevenly in her chest as she slowly reached into her pocket and brought out a few sugar lumps, which she always carried in her riding jacket.

The mare snorted suspiciously, every muscle tense, ready to leap away if Angel went too far. Angel very slowly extended her hand out to her. "Go ahead," she encouraged softly, as the mare tentatively stretched her slender neck towards her. Angel was quivering inside with excitement as the mare took the sugar, still alert, reading Angel's every move. "I will call you... Jewel," she smiled, keeping her tone soft and quietening. Wouldn't it be great to see her father's expression when he saw her riding home on the back of this beautiful horse, which he didn't even believe existed! If only she could... She took a small step towards her, but that was the step too far, and the mare, Jewel, pressed her ears back and reared before taking off into the blizzard. Angel made an effort to follow but was beaten back by the wind and snow. What chance did she think she had, anyway? She cursed and could only stand helplessly at the cave mouth and stare out into the blizzard.

When it was apparent that her precious Jewel was not going to return, Angel walked over to inspect the wall of the cave and frowned. It was bone dry again. Well, she couldn't have imagined it, because her back was still very wet. Yet what had she expected? Being a scientifically minded person, all this lack of logic was very disturbing. She was beginning to realise that nothing about this cave, or indeed the mare, could be taken for granted. She racked her brains for an explanation. Maybe this mare was some figment of her imagination. Maybe she was psychologically disturbed. Maybe she wasn't even here, maybe she was dreaming again! Nothing she could come up with could calm her mind. Shivering again, Angel sat back down, curling herself up into the tightest ball she could in an attempt to get warm.

★

The storm was at its height when the mare returned. Angel had temporarily dozed off but awoke to find herself in the same insane situation, and gasped as she saw the mare standing watching her. She slowly stood up. "I'm not going to hurt you," she reassured. This time Angel made no attempt to approach her, testing her own self-control. Jewel stood fast, and so began the battle of wills to see who would crack first. The mare stretched out her nose again, obviously begging for another lump of sugar, but Angel didn't move. "You've gotta come and get it."

Jewel snorted with frustration, and Angel had to fight to stop herself laughing at her. Then, at last, she took a step forward, still extending her quivering nostrils to Angel's hand. Angel smiled with relief as the mare allowed her to run her hand along her nose, and up to rub her snowy velvet ears. "You see, that's not so bad."

As she looked into Jewel's large, kind eyes, Angel noticed a feint tint of blue, which was strangely familiar to her. It was a fleeting thought and quickly dismissed.

Jewel nibbled at the pocket of Angel's jacket.

"Gee, you're persistent!" giggled Angel and relented. "Now, are we friends?" Her touch no longer freaked Jewel out. She even showed small signs of enjoyment as Angel continued to pet her. She moved from her ears, down her neck and onto her withers, until Angel could control herself no longer and vaulted up onto the mare's back.

Having weight on her back was obviously something new and extremely frightening for Jewel and she flipped. Angel was used to riding rodeo from when they had to break horses in on the ranch. Sure, she was used to a bridle and saddle to help her stay on, but, as she saw it, this horse was worth the risk of being thrown. She just grabbed on to the long, flowing mane and held on for dear life, constantly speaking softly to her in an attempt to calm her down more quickly.

They raced out into the snow, twisting and leaping, until at last gradually the mare quietened. Angel was surprised to find herself still on Jewel's back. She had been tossed around like one of the snowflakes and was briefly quite disorientated. But she smiled. "It's OK," she comforted, reaching forward to stroke Jewel's neck. Jewel threw her head in the air, still not at all comfortable with the situation. Angel grinned in triumph and attempted to turn her in the direction of home; but Jewel was not ready to submit to the will of any rider, even if she did have an endless supply of sugar! Her own will was too strong, and she took off again, this time heading straight for the cave.

Angel soon realised that they were going too fast to stop in time. Her efforts to slow Jewel down only made her go faster. She leant right forward, tucking her head down under her arms and tightened her grip on the mare's mane. She closed her eyes tightly, trying to prepare herself to be smashed into the wall. The mare took a gigantic leap and Angel screamed.

Equensia

Equensia

Much to her surprise, Angel found herself alive when she opened her eyes. She had indeed been thrown and the first thing she saw was the mare, disappearing into the trees. Then she gasped. She was sitting waist deep in an icy pool. For a few agonising seconds she couldn't move. Then, with immense brainpower, she scrambled out onto the snowy bank. She was shivering uncontrollably as she stood up and scanned the area. Snow, trees, rocks, yet none were familiar to her. And even more puzzling, there was no blizzard. The air was crystal clear. She looked around again, suddenly experiencing a deep sense of foreboding. She had no idea where she was; no idea which way was home. She was lost and alone, and very, very cold.

Then, something caught her attention in the undergrowth at the edge of the trees; maybe a rabbit? Angel went over to investigate but found nothing, except for some tiny footprints, like those of a small child. Angel frowned. What was a baby doing out here all alone? Its parents must be somewhere, and they were trespassing! She followed the tracks in the snow for a long while. Surely she should have caught up with a toddler by now? It must have been fed on steroids!

As the light faded, Angel became hungry. She gave up on the trail and began to look for something to eat. She had seen no signs of any creatures at all, except for the bionic baby, so she started looking for berries, nuts or edible plants. Her father had taught her basic survival skills, but she was finding it very difficult. A lot of the plants she had never seen before, and when it came to berries, "if in doubt, don't" was a wise philosophy. She had doubts about them all! She became very discouraged, and as the sun set on that first day she found shelter in a giant hollow tree.

The first time she realised she was no longer on her own ranch was that first night. The noises that kept her awake were frightening to say the least; growls and howls that she could place to no living thing that she knew. She had never been so petrified in her life as when she watched something pass her tree in the pitch blackness. All she could see were the protruding canine teeth and the whites of the animal's eyes as it padded past, grunting quietly. It was about the size of a bear, but it was certainly no bear! Angel tucked her knees up under her chin, quivering with fear, scared to move in case whatever it was was still around. She managed to drop off to sleep just before dawn and was woken up not long afterwards by voices. She froze again as they got louder.

"Why don't you just fly up there?" said one, and they stopped in front of Angel's hiding place.

"I am *not* your slave!" replied a croaky, gruff voice. "Just because I have my wings now, that does not mean I have to fly for you!"

"Fine! We'll all just starve!" retorted the first voice. "What it *does* mean is that I get to order you around! Now climb up there and get me my breakfast!"

"Mandor, you're the smallest and the lightest. You could probably jump up there," suggested the first voice.

"Oh, no," said a timid, quite high-pitched voice. "What if... something could be up there? Oh no, I can't!"

"There's nothing up there. Except breakfast!"

"You say that now, but if you had seen that monster yesterday...!"

"Just get up that tree," ordered the gruff voice. "That's an order!"

"It was horrible," he went on, "with big black feet!" Angel heard scraping on the tree as he climbed up. "It chased me for miles. I'd never been so scared in my life!"

"I find that very hard to believe. Now watch your step or you'll fall!"

Just as the first voice said that, there was a shrill scream, and with a thud a little creature fell right at Angel's feet. Her eyes opened wide as she saw two small pink feet sticking out of the snow, kicking frantically. The same little feet that had made the tracks the day before, she guessed. It had a furry belly the size of a beach ball, and, as it sat up, she saw it looked like a miniature abominable snowman, with large, naked pink ears and enormous black eyes; very cute. As it struggled to its feet, it happened to touch one of Angel's riding boots and froze. Angel was just about to go out and introduce herself when the creature screamed hysterically. "Big black feet! It's the monster! Oh, no! Somebody save me! "

"Calm down," said one of his colleagues, grabbing his arm as he charged past, his feet still running, kicking up the snow.

"Run! Save yourselves!" he panicked, continuing to scream. "It'll eat us all! "

"Come out," ordered the voice, "very slowly."

"I'm not a monster," said Angel defensively.

"We'll be the judge of that. Come out."

Angel slowly emerged from inside the tree. One of the group was a boy; about her age, with shoulder length, messy brown hair and piercing green eyes. He was wearing what looked like a homemade suit of armour, made from tree bark, and sat on his shoulder was what looked like a blue, furry dragon, about the size of a cat. He was holding a wooden spear very threateningly.

"It's… a girl," he observed.

"Be careful," warned the dragon, whispering. "Could be sorcery. A trick."

"Where do you come from?"

"Er… I'm not really sure. Where am I?"

"You see! She's stalling!" said the dragon again; then to Angel. "We'll ask the questions, monster! Now, what are Jazzaar's plans?"

Angel frowned. "Who? And my name is Angel, not 'monster'."

"I think she's genuine," said the boy.

The dragon fluffed himself up until he looked like a furry pompom with legs and a face. "Fine!" he croaked sulkily. "Don't come running to me when she grows three heads!"

Angel frowned and asked again. "Where am I?"

"You're in the Fiery Forest, in the land of Equensia," replied the boy proudly. "It's my land. My father left it to me."

"For what it's worth!" mumbled the dragon, rather jealously.

"Just because you have your wings, that doesn't mean you rule the entire universe!" the boy snapped, offended.

"Then maybe you could help me," said Angel hopefully. "I'm looking for my horse."

Even Mandor – which was the white creature's name – who all this time had been trying to escape the boy's hold, looked at her shocked.

The boy frowned. "Horse?"

"Yes, a mare. A white mare."

"There is only one mare, and she belongs to me!" the boy warned.

"Oh, well you see, that's how I came to be here. I was riding her, and..." she paused, as there was an outburst of objections. "What?"

"*Nobody* rides the white mare!" exclaimed the boy. "I *own* her, and even I've never ridden her!"

Angel grinned. "You don't know what you're missing. She's wonderful!"

"No, you don't understand. No one has ever ridden her and no one ever will. You are mistaken."

Angel frowned, rather offended. "Excuse me, but just because you can't be bothered to ride her, that doesn't mean that no one else can. I assure you, I *did* ride her, and it was fantastic!"

"How dare you call me a liar!" accused the boy, furiously, and he lifted his spear as if to throw it at her. "Take it back!"

Angel staggered backwards with fright, tripping over a tree root.

"Jack, leave it," said the dragon, as the boy glared angrily at Angel. "She's just a foolish child who doesn't know what she's saying. Come on; let's leave her to her fantasies."

Angel watched them walk away for a while, before scrambling back to her feet. "Jack! Wait!"

He seemed surprised she knew his name.

She gave an exasperated sigh. "Maybe you're right. I've seen so many things these past two days that anything's possible. Please? I have a feeling I'm gonna need your help."

Jack turned around. "Well, that's more like it." And they carried on walking.

Angel stared after them, puzzled, until they stopped again.

"Well? Are you coming or not?"

Angel ran to catch up, smiling with relief. "So you will help me?"

"Help you what?"

"Catch my horse and get back home."

Jack glared at her again.

"I'm sorry. I understand how you feel. She is a beautiful horse, but all I know is I found her wondering around my dad's ranch, and as possession is nine tenths of the law, I figure that makes her ours."

"I don't care about your 'laws'!" sneered Jack. "The mare belongs to me. That's a fact; the only one that matters to me. I don't want to discuss it any further. I'll help you get home, wherever that is, but the mare stays with me!"

"OK, fine." Angel smiled secretly to herself, knowing that when she got back home her father would sue this kid and they would win back her precious Jewel. "So where would we find her?"

"She lives here, in the forest."

"Not running free? Not in winter? She'll freeze to death!"

"Maybe you're deaf! I said I don't want to discuss the mare any more!"

"I've named her Jewel..." smiled Angel, dreamily. "OK! Subject dropped!"

Jack sighed with annoyance.

"What is there to eat around here? I'm starving!"

"We were just about to have breakfast when you gave our harvester a heart attack. Mandor!" called Jack.

He had been keeping a fearful distance from Angel and peeped out from behind a tree.

"Come on! We're hungry!"

"So am I!" growled Angel, jokingly, causing Mandor to scream and hide again.

Both Jack and the dragon looked accusingly at Angel, who laughed. "I'm sorry! I couldn't resist it. Come on, Mandor," she called. "I was only kiddin'! I would never eat you. You're much too cute!" She smiled at him, quivering behind the tree. He eventually managed to find the courage to come out from his hiding place, after making Angel promise to keep her distance. "What species is he?" asked Angel, giggling as she watched him climbing the tree. He looked very comical, with his big belly swinging from side to side as he climbed.

"Who, Mandor? He's just a skrift," replied Jack.

"Not noted for their bravery!" added the dragon, with a hint of snobbery.

"And you're a dragon, aren't you?" guessed Angel.

"A dragon?" he objected, very offended.

"Fraz is a jabbott," informed Jack.

"A what?" Fraz warned.

"Sorry, a *flying* jabbott," Jack corrected quickly.

"Indeed." Fraz puffed out his chest proudly.

"Forgive my ignorance, but I've never heard of a skrift, or a jabbott; never mind a flying one!"

"Oh, Fraz didn't always fly," explained Jack,

"Please, don't remind me," Fraz interrupted, "I'm trying to put it behind me!"

"It takes years for a jabbott to acquire wings. Until then, they just crawl and climb."

"Belly-boshers!" jeered Fraz.

"It's when they get their wings that they think they're the ruler of everything and everything is below them," accused Jack.

"OK, mighty warrior, we'll see how long you last on your own," snapped Fraz and he took off.

"Don't you want any breakfast?" called Angel, rather worried.

"I'll get my own!" came the reply.

"And easily offended," added Jack.

60

"Shouldn't we go after him?"

"He'll be back," Jack was confident, and looked up the tree. Mandor had just reached the top. "What is it today?" he called up.

"Oranges again!"

"Again?" Jack exclaimed. "It's been oranges now for over a week!" He sighed. "OK," he called, "you may as well throw some down."

Angel frowned, puzzled yet again. "What do you mean? Surely an orange tree always produces oranges, doesn't it?"

"Probably, but this isn't an orange tree."

"Oh." Angel slowly shook her head. "I daren't ask."

"It's a peapor tree."

"Peapor?"

"Never heard of those either?" Jack guessed and sighed. "A peapor tree has pears one day, apples another, oranges another, you know? Depending on the mood of the tree?"

Angel sensed that Jack was getting fed up of explaining everything to her, so from then on (at least for a while) she kept her puzzlements to herself. They tucked in greedily to the oranges that Mandor threw down. However, one could only eat so many oranges at one time, so they packed the rest up in Jack's small carrying sack and set off again. Then, suddenly, Angel's heart leapt as she saw the now unmistakable snow flurry of the mare as she went prancing in and out of the trees. "There!" she exclaimed in excitement, and instinctively went to run after her, but Jack grabbed her arm. "Come on!" she persisted obsessively, trying to drag him with her.

"No!" he said, sharply.

"But that's her! That's my horse!"

"Wrong! That's *my* horse!" Jack was getting tired of having to remind her. "And I say leave her."

"But we've gotta catch her! She knows me now! Come on, I'll show you!"

But in their moment of hesitation, the mare had vanished again.

"Oh, no!" cried Angel in despair. "Why didn't you come? We may never get another chance! " She was almost catatonic.

"Don't worry," reassured Jack, somewhat calmer. "When she wants to, the mare will come to us."

"'When she wants to'," mumbled Angel under her breath. How stupid was that? She didn't believe him for a second. She stood and searched the trees again, desperate.

"Come on!" urged Jack.

Angel was desperate to go and look for tracks, but she followed, not wanting to be left on her own again.

"Why is Mandor still scared of me?" Angel wondered, watching him dodge nervously from tree to tree, keeping about fifty yards away from them. "I mean, do I really look like a monster?"

"Not to me," Jack replied. "But to a skrift, everything is a monster until proven otherwise."

"But how do I prove it?"

"Well, telling him how hungry you are is not likely to hold well in convincing him you're not going to eat him, is it?"

"True," she giggled.

"Give him time. He'll come round."

"I could understand it if I looked like that thing I saw last night. Now *that* was a monster! It was as tall as me and as black as night. Shaggy hair, and man! It smelt! And the teeth on this thing! I mean, they were at least three inches long!"

"You saw a Gragg?" Jack gasped in surprise.

"I don't know what it was, but I was scared, petrified!"

"And lucky," Jack added. "Most people who see a Gragg… well they don't get to see the dawn."

"Really? So you've never seen one then?"

Jack shook his head. "Don't want to either. I got attacked when I was a baby, but I was too young to remember. I only survived because of my father."

"Your father? Who was he?"

"He was a warrior. Some say he was the greatest warrior ever. I never knew him, or my mother. Fraz told me they disappeared while looking for the Gragg that attacked us. He raised me and looked after me."

"Do you know if they're still alive?"

Jack was becoming tense. It was obviously a painful subject for him.

"It's OK," comforted Angel. "I lost my mother too. I understand if you don't want to talk about it."

"They're both dead. I mean, it's obvious isn't it?"

"Does Fraz not know what happened to them?"

"He denies it. He says they're still alive somewhere; they just left. It's stupid. They wouldn't just leave! Fraz says they were cowards, but they couldn't have been. They were warriors, both of them!"

"Have you never tried to find out what really happened?"

"No. It wouldn't change anything. If they're dead, nothing will bring them back; and if they're just cowards, I don't want to know them anyway."

"That would drive me mad, not knowing," Angel thought out loud.

"Well it doesn't bother me, OK?" snapped Jack.

Angel knew he was just in denial; just afraid of the pain that was attached to losing a parent, a pain she knew all too well. "I'll help you."

"I don't need your help."

"It's the least I can do," she insisted. "You help me, I help you. Deal?"

"How about I help you and you leave?" Jack sighed at her hurt expression. "I'm sorry, look; we should rest here for a while. Fraz should be back soon. I'm going to fetch some firewood. You wait here."

"What if that… Gragg comes back?"

"You sound like Mandor!" he sniggered. "You'll be fine. The Gragg doesn't come out until after dark. We'll be hidden away long before then."

Hidden away? He made her feel like a hunted rabbit! Rabbits! That was what was missing! She hadn't seen any sign of rabbits, or birds, or anything like that since she got here. Where were all the small animals? "Mandor," she called. "Come here. I want to ask you something."

"*Ja–ack!*" he screamed, and sped off in the direction that Jack had gone.

Angel sighed. Was she ever going to win over the cute little skrift? She watched him waddling at top speed, with his arms flailing in the air in his panic. Then, almost immediately, the loneliness and the isolation began eating at her again. Also the fear of being completely vulnerable; ignorant of any dangers there might be. She was easy meat! She shivered and decided to climb up a tree where she might feel a bit safer.

However, she was not up to practice on her climbing skills. She tried her best to copy Mandor's climbing technique, but it was more difficult than it looked. She hadn't picked the best tree for climbing, either; with its smooth bark and vertical trunk. Still, she managed to reach the first of the leaves before coming face to face with Fraz.

"You're not very good at this, are you?" he observed.

Angel screamed, startled, and did what Mandor had done earlier that day – fell to earth with a thud. Luckily, the snow broke her fall. "Fraz!" she exclaimed with a certain degree of relief. "How long have you been there?"

"Long enough," replied the voice in the leaves, and he sprang out of the tree, landing lightly on a snow-covered stump. "I've been following for a while. Jack needs me more than he will admit to. It's up to me to look out for him. He thinks he's a warrior, but the truth is, without me he wouldn't last five minutes."

"Jack was right about one thing. You really do think you rule the universe!"

"I guess I should expect nothing more from a child like you. But the truth is the truth. Whether you like it or not!" And he flew back up into the tree.

Easily offended too, Angel thought to herself and sniggered, then turned back to look up into the tree. "Tell me about Jack's parents?"

Fraz suddenly swooped down out of the tree and Angel staggered backwards as he hovered in front of her. "There's nothing to tell. They're cowards. They left. End of story!"

Angel frowned at his offensive tone. "For someone who talks a lot about the truth, that's rather hypocritical. I intend to find out the real truth about what happened to them. It's only fair to Jack. He deserves to know."

"Well, you'll never find out from me. You *don't* deserve it!"

"Fine," she replied defiantly, "but I *will* find out!"

"Believe me," said Fraz, a little calmer, "you have no idea what you're heading for if you persist with this. Trust me; forget it. Jack's happy. He doesn't need this."

"He might seem happy to you, but he's tortured inside. I know how it feels to lose a parent. I can see he's hurting too. So I'm gonna help him. It seems strange to me that his so-called 'friends' are unwilling to do the same."

"If your ideas weren't so foolish, I would consider them courageous. But they *are* foolish. You don't know what you're dealing with."

"So tell me," Angel persisted.

Fraz paused. "Jack's parents are gone. Gone for good. Jack has accepted that. You should too."

But all Fraz had succeeded in doing was arousing Angel's curiosity even more. And once aroused, it would not diminish.

The Gragg

The Gragg

ack returned not long afterwards with an armful of firewood. Angel knew the loss of his parents was a tense subject so let it drop, but her brain was working overtime trying to think up a plan; some means of squeezing information out of the stubborn jabbott. The only thing that could take her mind off such a difficult task was food, and she grinned as she saw Jack also had a few creatures that he had caught. They looked a lot like large rats, but with the same protruding teeth as the Gragg. In fact, they could well have been baby Graggs. Miniature monsters! Angel gasped in terror and scrambled back, bumping into a tree.

Jack laughed and waved them in front of her. "It's OK, look! They're dead!"

Angel tried to tell him, but the words caught in her throat and the only sound she could make was a pathetic whimper.

Fraz also seemed concerned.

"What's wrong with everyone? I caught lunch!"

"Where exactly did you find them?" asked Fraz.

"Well…" mused Jack, "they were asleep. All together."

"Alone?" Fraz questioned, becoming increasingly worried.

"Yeah."

"You found a Gragg's nest?"

"A Gragg?"

"Do you know what you've done?" Fraz was hysterical. "You stupid child! You've raided a Gragg's nest and killed its cubs!"

"All the more reason to celebrate! Three less Graggs!"

"The parent will be furious!"

"Ah! Poor thing," defended Jack sarcastically.

"Don't you understand? Everybody knows you don't just kill a Gragg's offspring! It will hunt you down relentlessly!"

"So we'll just go to the hideout." Jack still didn't know what all the fuss was about.

"We can't. You have the smell all over you."

"So, we'll wash in the waterfall."

"The smell won't just wash off!"

"I'll vouch for that," said Angel.

Sure enough, they heard the ferocious growl echo around the forest. The Gragg had returned to its empty nest.

"It'll be coming!" panicked Fraz.

"So what do we do?" Jack was quickly sobering up.

"*We?*" Fraz flew up into the tree. "Who's we? It's you it's after!"

Jack quickly threw the young Graggs at the foot of the tree and picked up his spear, saying, "Well, I guess there's only one thing to do."

"Come on, Fraz! You said you were here to look out for him," reminded Angel, "so help him!"

"That child is beyond help!"

"It sounds to me like you're the coward!" she accused and, though trembling with fear, she stood next to Jack, prepared to fight alongside him. "This is stupid," she sang quietly through her teeth, all the time hearing the Gragg's vicious growls as it followed their scent, focused and determined. "Jack, what are we doing?"

"We can't run; we can't hide. What else is there?"

"We could try and lead it somewhere. Make it difficult to follow the trail. Slow it down to give us some time to think a way around it. Anything's better than just waiting here!"

"That would just prolong it. You don't have to stay. As Fraz said, it's me it wants."

"And you think it will stop after killing you?"

"I'm hoping to put an end to it before it gets to that stage. Honestly, I appreciate it, but it's not your fight."

"You need all the *help* you can get," hinted Angel, glaring angrily into the tree.

"If you had an ounce of intelligence, you'd do as he says," Fraz called back.

"I can't believe you're just going to stand there and watch him get torn to pieces. Some friend you are!"

"Hey," objected Jack, "nobody's gonna get torn to pieces, OK!"

Suddenly, with a terrifying roar, the Gragg came in sight. It was even more horrifying in the daylight.

"Is that…"

71

"A Gragg?" Angel finished off his sentence for him, as he was obviously unable to speak through pure dread. She nodded her head and flattened herself against the trunk of the tree.

Jack immediately realised he had grossly over-estimated himself and stood paralysed with fear as the creature approached. "My... dad... fought... *that*?" he stammered. His arm fell limp at his side and the spear fell to the floor.

"Jack!" whispered Angel, trying to break him out of his terror-induced trance. "Come on. Your dad could do it; so can you. You've got to!"

"It's over," he said hopelessly.

"Jack, come on!" Angel repeated more urgently, becoming increasingly terrified herself as the Gragg continued to advance. With another angry roar, Angel looked one more time up into the tree. "Please," she begged. "Do something!"

Fraz was tortured – torn between his own self-preservation and saving Jack, the only family he had left. When Jack's father – Fraz's previous master – had fought the Gragg, he had not needed his help. He had been a fully-fledged warrior and therefore he had insisted Fraz stay a safe distance away. However, Jack was foolish and over-confident. He was just a boy. He didn't stand a chance. But still, what could one flying jabbott do against a Gragg? The situation seemed hopeless. Fraz took a deep breath, fluffing up his chest fur proudly as he came to a decision. If they were all going to die anyway, which was an overwhelming probability, then he would rather die proving he was not a coward. So he spread his wings, for probably the last time, and began his suicidal flight.

"Fraz!" Jack tried to call him back, but he was focused; his mind was made up.

"Oh, no," said Angel quietly, realising what he was doing. "Come on, Jack; we've gotta help him!"

Fraz hovered briefly above the Gragg, but not long enough to have second thoughts, and dived onto the creature's back. He clung on desperately to the shaggy hair with his long, strong claws and, trying to ignore the unbearable stench, he sank his teeth into its neck.

The Gragg let out a stomach-churning scream of pain and fury, trying everything it could to shake off this irritant.

Jack snatched up his spear and sped towards them, yelling, trying to frighten it off, or even aiming to kill it while it was distracted.

Fraz knew his survival depended on how long he was able to hang on. But his jaws were aching and his feet were slipping. Inevitably, the Gragg shook itself free and grabbed him in its jaws, shaking its head viciously before throwing him against a tree.

"No!" yelled Jack, and with speed and strength that only comes from rage, he drove the spear deep into the Gragg's side, provoking another of those screams. The Gragg swiped at him, but he was just out of reach. Jack stabbed again; another scream. He had found himself in the same situation as Fraz: as long as he was able to stay on one end of the spear, and keep the Gragg on the other end, he was safe and unreachable. He jabbed again and again. Why wouldn't this creature die? If he had stabbed a few inches across he would have pierced its heart but, in his fury, he had not bothered to aim. All he could do now was hope to wear it down. The snow underfoot had already been stained red, and with each new stab Jack could tell it was weakening. All he had to do was hang on until it bled to death.

"Hey!" called Angel suddenly, holding up the dead babies tauntingly.

"Angel, no!" yelled Jack as the Gragg roared furiously.

"Are you looking for these?" she jeered, but swallowed hard as the Gragg began to drag Jack towards her. He did his best to hold it back, but even in its weakened state it was still too strong and determined for him.

"Angel, what are you doing?" He strained. Under such pressure the spear snapped and Jack fell backwards. The Gragg saw the opportunity and took it, swiping out at him again, slicing his ribs, even through his armour. It was just about to finish him off when Angel distracted it again.

"Hey, come on! This is what you want!"

The Gragg growled, and with one more look at Jack, it turned towards Angel. She smiled, knowing she had succeeded in taking its attention off Jack, but at the same time she became aware of how unbelievably stupid she was. "Er… Jack?" she whispered over to him. "What do I do, Jack?"

He lay motionless, face down in the snow.

"Two down, one to go," she mumbled under her breath, as the Gragg held her mercilessly in its furious glare. Her heart was pounding so fast Angel thought she was going to pass out; she wished she *could* pass out! And with another hopeful glance towards Jack, she threw one of the dead babies at the Gragg. She had no idea what she was hoping to achieve. The Gragg stopped and sniffed at the little body, nudging it with its nose, hoping it would respond. When there was no response, the Gragg roared furiously at Angel. She had only succeeded in making it angrier. She threw the other two. The Gragg checked each one to see if either was alive, but found that both were indeed dead, and its anger erupted.

Angel squashed herself up against a tree and closed her eyes tightly, preparing herself to be eaten alive, when there was a sudden rush of wind. She quickly opened her eyes to see the mare leap right over the Gragg, and as she landed she lashed out with both of her hind legs, knocking the Gragg sliding through the snow. Angel gasped in amazement as she watched Jewel rear up and squeal, trampling the baby Graggs into the snow, as if to purposefully anger the Gragg; and before it had really regained its senses, she struck out again. Then, with a gigantic buck, she raced off into the forest, with the furious Gragg (still with half a spear sticking out of its side) hard on her heels.

★

It was a while before Angel found she could breathe properly again, and she went over to check on Jack. She saw a flicker of pain in his face as she turned him over and sighed with relief. At least he was still alive. She glanced over to where Fraz was still lying motionless at the foot of the tree. There was no way he could still be alive. The way the Gragg had shaken him; he would have been killed almost instantly. Guilt began to eat at her and she started to cry. The cuts on Jack's ribs were bleeding heavily. If she didn't do something he wouldn't survive much longer either.

Angel jumped, startled as Mandor came up behind her. "Where did you disappear to?"

"Someone had to fetch the mare," he pointed out.

"Fraz is dead," she sniffed. "It's all my fault. Jack's bleeding to death. I don't know what to do. I wish my dad was here."

"Those are empty wishes. He's not here. It's just us. Lambin leaves will stop the bleeding." Mandor waddled off, presumably to collect the leaves.

"What should I do?" asked Angel, desperate to help and feeling responsible for everything that had happened.

"Don't ask me, I'm just a skrift! Wait here. Try and keep him warm."

Angel quickly took off her wax jacket and wrapped it around Jack. "Its gonna be OK," she said, reassuring herself as much as Jack.

Mandor soon returned with about a dozen of the large lime-green leaves. "First, we'll have to move him somewhere safe," said Mandor. "Do you think you can carry him?"

"Well, there's no one else, is there? I'll have to. Where are we going?"

"There's a cave, behind a waterfall. I go there when there's danger."

Angel smiled to herself. It looked like Mandor was starting to see her as something other than a monster.

She lifted Jack up and put his arm around her shoulders. He was very heavy. "Is it far?"

"Quite a way," he replied. "We can rest on the way. But the Gragg will return here for its cubs. We can't stay."

"What about Fraz?"

Mandor looked back towards him, and slowly shook his head.

"Shouldn't we bury him?"

"We don't have time. The Gragg could return any minute. Trust me. We have to go."

Angel looked regretfully back and struggled on.

★

They walked for hours through the silent forest. The only sound was that of the wind whistling through a hollow tree. Angel forced herself, though exhausted, to go further and further, until she collapsed, unable to stumble another step.

"We haven't got far to go," encouraged Mandor.

"I'm sorry, Mandor," she panted. "I need to rest for just a little while."

Mandor looked fearfully around. "Well, OK. Just for a while."

Angel lay Jack down again and flopped against a tree, completely exhausted.

Mandor pulled the shoulder strap off the carrying sack and used it to tie the lambin leaves tightly onto Jack's wounds.

Worryingly, Angel noticed no flinch in his face like before. He was completely unconscious, though still alive.

"There," said Mandor as he finished dressing the wounds. "All we need to do now is get him to the hideout, and he'll be fine."

Angel wished she could share his optimism. The way she saw it, Jack was getting worse, not better, and was probably dying. And her only other companion was a skrift who, though unbelievably cute, would run a mile at the first hint of danger. She was never going to get home. At least at home her problems were normal! Here, she had no idea where she was, where she was going or what she had to do to get back. The only person whom she felt could help her find out was Jack. If he died, she had a sickening feeling that she was going to be stuck here forever!

Mandor sensed her deflation. "Everything will be OK," he reassured.

"Huh!" Angel scoffed. "How d'you figure?"

He smiled. "Wherever it is you came from, the mare goes there regularly. She'll help."

Angel's hopes soared again. "How do you know?"

"She told me, of course!"

"You can speak to her?"

"Sure! We skrifts can speak to every animal in the forest." He paused. "Well, we used to. The mare is the only one I talk to now."

"Why?"

He sniggered at the question. "Because she is the only one who doesn't want to eat me! Have you ever tried to hold a conversation with a Gragg?"

"But that's not the only creature in the forest, is it?"

"Of course not, but…" Mandor paused again. "You really don't know, do you."

"Know what?"

He stood up. "Let's go."

"Come on, Mandor," begged Angel, desperately.

"Later. We're in danger here. The hideout's not far from here."

Angel reluctantly heaved Jack up again and they set off once more.

"Wait here," said Mandor after a while and he waddled ahead. He cautiously peeped out through the thick leaves and scanned the clearing. It looked deserted. But experience had taught him never to judge by appearances and he crept out, scouring the snow for the slightest tracks. There were a few, but they were all hours old. All was well, so he went to fetch Angel and Jack. They were waiting for him patiently where he had left them. "Come on," he beckoned. "It's all clear."

Angel gasped as she reached the edge of the clearing and looked down into the valley. There she saw the most beautiful waterfall.

"Come on!" he persisted impatiently. "Be careful here," he warned, climbing carefully around the side of the small lagoon and disappearing behind the wall of water.

Angel struggled to follow him. The rocks were extremely slippery. She almost lost her footing more than once, but just managed to get herself and Jack behind the waterfall, and at last she was able to rest again.

She spread her jacket over the cold, wet rock to act as a makeshift bed for Jack. She stood back and looked around for the first time, and saw that they had got quite a cosy little home here, with a generous supply of firewood in one corner. A few spears and a bow with arrows stood against the back wall. A spare suit of armour, a hollow wooden stump full of apples, pears and oranges, and what looked like the skin of a wolf hung on the wall. There was also another stump of wood, carved in the shape of a chair. Mandor was busy lighting a fire.

Angel had not forgotten their previous conversation and was just picking her moment to bring up the subject again. She strolled around the small cave, inspecting their new accommodation. "Is this a wolf skin?" she asked, letting her fingers run through the luxurious thick fur of the rug hanging on the wall.

Mandor glanced up briefly from his consuming task of fire making. "That was Jack's first successful hunt. He's really proud of that."

"I can see why," replied Angel, as she spotted the two-inch-long, talon-like claws, which were still attached to the legs. "He is very brave."

"He was mad!" retorted Mandor. "You should have seen it! It nearly killed him!"

"Like the Gragg?"

"Worse! He was younger then too; too young to be going hunting. But Fraz always wanted him to be the brave warrior. Like his father was."

"You knew his parents?" Angel's eyes lit up.

"Sure! It was Jack's grandfather who rescued me."

"From what?"

Mandor frowned suspiciously. "Are you *sure* you're not working for Jazzaar?"

Angel was frustrated. "Why is it no one will explain to me about anything? What is everyone afraid of?"

Mandor eventually sighed and relented. "It's a long story. You'd better sit down."

Angel sat on the chair stump, feeling rather excited.

Mandor still kept her in suspense a little longer. She sat patiently waiting until he had succeeded in lighting a fire. Angel had forgotten what it felt like to be warm and closed her eyes blissfully as the warmth reached her.

"What's wrong?" frowned Mandor, prepared to flee if she was about to shed her skin and transform into her true, hideous, monstrous form.

"Nothin'. It's just… wonderful." She paused. "The heat."

"Oh."

"Carry on."

"Well, as I said before, it was Jack's grandfather who rescued me. I was running from this monster. It was hideous! I fell into a ditch and suddenly there were monsters everywhere! Monsters on the left, monsters on the right. I was surrounded! I really thought I'd had it…"

Angel saw the fear in his eyes. He was reliving the whole story as he was telling it.

"…They put me in a cage. I kept telling them: 'Why don't you eat me?' But they wouldn't. I wished they would! I was so scared; I thought I was going to have a heart attack! It was then they took me to Wystrazura."

"Are you OK?" asked Angel. Mandor seemed to be in a trance, with a permanent expression of terror on his face. "Where's Wystrazura?"

"Wystrazura is the most evil, terrifying place of demons and monsters. It is the fortress of Jazzaar; a powerful sorcerer. I hope you never have to meet him. People have looked into his eyes and turned to dust, or been possessed – gone mad. I would have come to the same fate if it hadn't been for Jack's grandparents."

"Did they kill him?"

"Kill him? There's not a force in the land that can kill Jazzaar! He's too powerful! I was lucky. Jack's grandfather Lucius rescued me before all the other prisoners were sacrificed. Even with the Willowand, all Jack's parents could do was confine him to Wystrazura."

"What's a Willowand? Some kind of stick or staff?"

"No, it's a belt. It makes the wearer invincible. It gives them powers which they wouldn't normally have. Jazzaar would do anything to get possession of it. Not because he needs it, but if he had it then no one would have the power to challenge him. That is why Lucius stole it in the first place."

"Where is this belt now?"

"No one knows. After killing the rest of Lucius's family, Jazzaar sent a Gragg to kill Jack's parents and retrieve the Willowand. It nearly killed Jack, but Maxus and Sonia, Jack's parents, distracted it just in time and led it off. They never returned. Jack was only a baby then. Jazzaar was furious when his monsters failed to find Maxus and the Willowand, and that's when he froze the seasons."

"Froze the seasons?"

"It's been winter now for twelve years."

Angel frowned. "But why? Why would he do that?"

"To flush Jack's father out. Think about it. All the creatures that breed in the spring haven't bred for twelve years. A lot of them have already died out. Plus, the animals that depend on grass and greenery for food have all starved. Jazzaar thought extinction on that scale would surely force him out of hiding. But he's never returned."

"Twelve years? That's a long time to hold a grudge!"

Mandor nodded, and glanced over at Jack, still unconscious. "We're all worried now that he'll try and take it out on Jack. Fraz did his best to teach him to fight, but without the Willowand, even the best warriors wouldn't have a chance against Jazzaar."

"What do you think happened to him?"

"All I know is that his disappearance can't be the work of Jazzaar, because of the way he reacted when he disappeared. And he wouldn't just leave his son."

"Do you think the Gragg got him?"

"Who knows? He was wearing the Willowand that day, so I doubt it. Whatever happened, it was his own choice."

"That explains Fraz's attitude to them."

"Fraz knew Jack's parents better than anyone. He'd been with them for over twenty-five years."

"He's gonna miss him, isn't he," said Angel, looking sympathetically at Jack. Mandor went over to check his ribs. Jack groaned as he began to come round. Angel quickly joined Mandor at his side.

"Fraz?" Jack mumbled.

"It's Mandor," he replied, softly. "Don't worry. You're safe; we're in the hideout."

"You're gonna be OK," Angel smiled, relieved to see him wake up, and she glanced over at Mandor. Even though he had told her a lot, she still had a feeling that he was keeping something from her. It would seem that there was more to this place than she could ever have thought.

★

Meanwhile, deep in the forest, the Gragg had given up chasing the mare. Once again she had escaped, and the Gragg returned exhausted to the scene of the day's battle. After once again checking its cubs, it found the patch of bloodstained snow where Jack had fallen and stared in the direction of the tracks which Angel had left when she carried him off into the forest. It was exhausted, almost to the point of collapsing, still bleeding heavily and snarling in frustration, knowing it didn't have the strength and energy to track them down and finish them off. So it turned around and walked over to where Fraz was still lying, and picking him up in its formidable jaws, it carried him off into the gloom.

The Betrayal

The Betrayal

"*Shavixi Degero Vinovo! Shavixi Degero Vinovo! Actum!* Ye–es; wake, my little furry friend."

Fraz's eyes flickered open. It took a while for him to figure out where he was. "Jazzaar," he croaked.

"It's been a long time."

"Not long enough."

Jazzaar laughed. "How about showing your resurrector a bit of gratitude?"

"I would rather be dead!"

"That can be arranged!" Jazzaar shouted furiously.

"I see your temper is as bad as ever." As his senses gradually returned, Fraz became aware that he was physically tied by chains on his legs to a metal hoop imbedded in rock. "This is a bit primitive, don't you think?"

"Primitive, but necessary. I see you've... matured."

Fraz quickly folded his wings out of sight.

"Now, don't be modest..." Jazzaar hooked his long index finger under Fraz's wing and outstretched it. "Impressive," he smirked.

"What do you want with me?" Fraz quickly turned his head away to avoid looking into Jazzaar's snake-like eyes and closed his own eyes tightly as he felt the sharp nail under his chin, turning his head to face him.

"Look into my eyes," Jazzaar instructed, his voice almost at a whisper.

"Not likely!" replied Fraz stubbornly.

"Do you really think you have the power to resist me?"

Fraz didn't answer; just closed his eyes even tighter.

Jazzaar gave an evil grin. "It seems you still have that stubborn streak. Excellent! It's been a long time since I last had some fun!" He took hold of Fraz's wing again, and his fingernail burnt through the thin membrane and sliced down.

Fraz tried to ignore the unbearable burning, and kept his eyes tightly shut.

"Where's Maxus?" he demanded after slicing poor Fraz's wing into strips.

"If I knew, do you really think I would tell you?" Fraz could hardly talk. "You're mad. You can do anything to me."

"That's exactly right! I can!" Jazzaar was losing his patience. "I can keep you alive while I remove your heart. Where is the Willowand?"

"Maxus or the Willowand? Make up your mind!" Fraz forced out a jeering snigger.

"It is not wise to taunt me," threatened Jazzaar.

"You're wasting your time," Fraz pointed out. "You'll never get any information out of me. Torture me all you like."

"I would love to, believe me, but I think you're right. And time is pressing."

Fraz gave a discreet sigh of relief, but then the darkest dread filled him as Jazzaar continued: "Go and fetch the boy."

"Jack?" Fraz whimpered.

"Oh, yes!" grinned Jazzaar, realising his plan was working. "Let's see how strong you are when the young warrior comes to play with me!"

"You don't have Jack." Fraz tried to convince himself.

"Ooh! Have we found a weakness?"

Fraz longed to open his eyes to see for himself if Jack had really been captured. He knew if it was true he would have to do what Jazzaar wanted. He couldn't risk Jack being killed. Sure enough, he heard chains and Jack's voice: "Fraz! Help me!"

"Jack!" he exclaimed, still with his eyes tightly closed.

"Fraz, please! Help me!"

"Enough talk!" said Jazzaar. "Now remember; this is only because you have such stubborn friends. I take no pleasure in torturing children. I want you to remember that."

"Fraz!" screamed Jack's voice again.

Fraz couldn't take it any more. "OK!" He opened his eyes to find Jazzaar face to face with him, staring straight at him. "Jack?" Fraz was confused.

Jazzaar stood up straight, laughing. "Fraz! Help me!" he jeered, doing a perfect impression of Jack's voice. "Not bad, eh?" he laughed again, and then became serious.

Fraz realised he had been tricked. He also realised he was doomed. Once Jazzaar had him in his stare, there was no escape.

Sure enough, Jazzaar outstretched his arms and his eyes glazed over with the blackness that would soon consume him. "*Kinjasurpo Habito Demaan!*" he chanted repeatedly. Though the spell was softly spoken, the words seared through Fraz's eyes, burning his brain and he was helpless to stop it. Jazzaar continued chanting until Fraz was completely possessed, practically reduced to a zombie. When he had stopped, Fraz collapsed with two trails of blood trickling from his eyes, like tears. With a flick of his wrist, Jazzaar freed Fraz from the chains and he slowly got to his feet. "You're mine," he smiled.

"Yes, master," replied Fraz.

★

Meanwhile, back at the hideout Jack had completely regained consciousness.

"You must remain still," insisted Mandor as Jack tried to get up.

"I've got to see about Fraz." Jack was determined.

"Mandor's right," said Angel. "You stay here and rest. We'll go."

"No!" said Mandor and Jack together. "It will be dark soon," Mandor went on. "It's too dangerous."

Jack cursed as he was forced to sit back down.

"Jeez! Look, you're bleeding again," fussed Mandor, urging him to lie down.

Jack sighed with frustration as Mandor put fresh lambin leaves on his ribs.

"Get some sleep." Mandor turned to Angel. "I'll take the first watch. I'll wake you at midnight."

Angel didn't need telling twice. She was exhausted, and lay down on the cold rock by the fire and immediately fell into a deep, dreamless sleep. As he looked from Angel to Jack, Mandor realised how vulnerable they were. Angel was obviously very naïve about the dark forces that held this winter land in its grip and Jack was still far from ready to take his father's place as warrior. They were both still just children. All skrifts had highly tuned senses and intuition and every sense was telling Mandor that something was coming. He didn't need senses to know Jazzaar wouldn't wait until Jack was old enough to pose a threat to him, no matter how small; but whatever he was planning, it was close – terrifyingly close. He shuddered, trying to stem the panic that rose within him.

Looking again at Angel, still fast asleep, Mandor realised that Angel may have to know the whole truth before she was ready to hear it; but not tonight. She had had as much as she could take in for one day. He let her sleep past midnight before gently waking her. "Your watch," he said, softly.

Angel stretched and yawned. For the first time, she was not alarmed or startled by what she saw when she opened her eyes. Maybe she was getting used to this place. She sat on the chair as Mandor settled down to sleep. "Wake me if you hear anything," he instructed.

"Be sure of it!" she replied, rather nervously; though she wasn't as scared as she had been on the previous night. She felt safer here, in the hideout.

As Mandor fell asleep, Angel's thoughts drifted to home. Dad would be going out of his mind by now. She wondered whether Wirlwind had got back safely or not; and Clare! Why hadn't she made up with her before going out riding that Tuesday morning? What if she never made it back home? Clare would spend the rest of her life thinking Angel hated her! If only for that reason, she had to get back home. Maybe Mandor was right and the mare intended to help her. She hoped so. She also thought about everything Mandor had told her about Jack's parents, the warriors, and the powerful Jazzaar. She hoped she would get home before having to meet him!

It was dawn when Fraz got to the hideout. Mandor was out collecting more lambin leaves. Angel was left to look after Jack; a task which only really involved guarding him in case he tried to get up. He was very impatient. Jack saw him first. "Fraz!" he exclaimed with relief, trying to spring to his feet, but Angel held him down. They both stared at Fraz as if he was a ghost. An understandable reaction, he thought.

"I've made it!" he panted and collapsed.

"You were dead." Angel was suspicious.

"Almost, but not quite."

"Obviously!" said Jack. "What happened to you?"

Fraz had had plenty of time to prepare answers to these inevitable questions. Convincing Jack and Angel was relatively easy. Mandor, however, was a different story. He was able to see the change in him straight away.

"Mandor, look who's back!" enthused Jack, when he returned with an armful of leaves.

Mandor froze.

"It's Fraz," reminded Angel.

Mandor shook his head. "No. Oh, no. That's not Fraz."

"What are you talking about? Of course it is! Look!"

"It is," said Fraz. "It's me."

Mandor dropped the leaves and sped off, screaming.

"I was afraid this might happen," said Fraz, dejectedly.

"It's OK," reassured Jack. "He thought you were dead; we all did."

"I'll go after him," suggested Angel.

"It won't do any good," said Fraz. "Once he's in a panic, he won't let anything near him. Best leave him to come back on his own."

Angel was unsure, but obeyed.

"So how did you get away?" asked Fraz, inspecting Jack's wounds. "Looks like you only just made it too!"

"Yeah." Jack smiled at Angel. "Angel distracted it. I managed to get a spear into it too."

"If I hadn't distracted it, the spear probably wouldn't have broke, and you would have been able to kill it," said Angel, regretfully. "And if I hadn't been nagging Fraz, he'd probably be OK too."

"He is OK!" insisted Jack. "We're all still alive, so everything's OK!"

Angel sighed, sympathetically examining Fraz's shredded wing. "How did this happen? You look like you've been tortured."

Fraz defensively snatched back his wing and hopped up onto a stump. "It's fine!" he snapped. "No thanks to you!"

"Fraz?" frowned Jack.

"No, she's right! None of this would have happened if it wasn't for her! I say Mandor was right! She is a monster, and we should treat her as such!" he grabbed the spear off the wall.

"No!" objected Jack, as Angel, hurt and frightened, stumbled out of the cave and through the waterfall. She ran as fast as she could across the clearing and into the forest.

Fraz smirked secretly to himself in triumph.

"Fraz!" scolded Jack. "How could you say that? She was only trying to help. Now go after her and apologise!"

"I will *not!*" he frowned. "Has it occurred to you that she might have planned all this so you'd be left alone and defenceless? We were all fine until she showed up!"

Jack frowned, confused. Angel couldn't have planned him getting injured, could she? It was impossible. But Fraz had successfully planted the seed of doubt in his mind, and he smirked again. "Believe me," he went on. "We're better off without her."

★

Angel ran herself to exhaustion, with tears streaming down her face. She stumbled over the root of a tree and fell face down, right next to one of the dead baby Graggs at the scene of the previous day's battle. Mandor was there with the mare, who reared up startled.

"It's OK." Mandor put his hand on her leg and she calmed down. "What happened?" he asked.

"No!" Angel scrambled back, as Mandor and The mare approached her. "Stay back! You don't want to know me! I'm jinxed! It's all my fault!"

"What are you talking about? What's your fault?"

"Everything! Jack getting hurt; Fraz getting hurt!"

"Fraz was killed," Mandor interrupted.

"There, you see! Jinxed!"

"You don't understand. Fraz really was dead. Come on, I'll show you."

Angel slowly got to her feet, her eyes suddenly fixed on the mare again. She whinnied nervously and Mandor swiftly turned to Angel.

"What?" she asked.

"She's worried in case you try and ride her again."

"What?" Angel repeated, frowning.

"Just don't try and ride her, OK?"

"OK." Angel was transfixed by the mare's beauty.

"Promise?"

"I promise."

Mandor touched the mare's leg again. "It's OK," he said, softly; then to Angel, "Come on." He showed her the tracks of the Gragg returning the previous evening, picking up Fraz's body and carrying it off. "The tracks are heading towards Wystrazura," he concluded. "And there is only one with the power to bring him back to life…"

"Jazzaar?" Angel guessed, fearfully.

Mandor nodded. "Precisely."

"But surely Fraz would never work for Jazzaar?" Angel thought out loud. "From what you tell me, Fraz has always been loyal to Jack and his parents. Why would he change sides now?"

"Maybe Jazzaar has some sort of mind control over him. There's got to be something. There's no telling what he's capable of." Mandor suddenly paused. "Where is Jack?"

"He's still back at the hideout..." Angel's voice trailed off.

"Alone? With Fraz?"

They all set off for the hideout as fast as they could. The mare galloped ahead. Angel was still exhausted, but forced herself to keep up with Mandor. If anything happened to Jack while she was away, she would never forgive herself. The mare stayed hidden at the edge of the trees to wait for Angel and Mandor.

"Wait!" said Mandor, skidding to a halt alongside the mare.

"What?" panted Angel.

"It will be better if we stay here, out of sight."

"Mandor, come on. Jack's in danger. I know you're scared; so am I, but we've gotta help him!"

"No, it's not that. If we wait here and watch, Fraz will think he's succeeded in getting Jack on his own. We wait for him to make his move, whatever it is. Besides, Fraz has been with Jack all his life. He's not going to believe us. If we go bursting in there, he's really going to push us away."

Angel knew he was right, so they waited, and waited, and waited, taking turns to watch for any signs of movement. Angel became worried as night fell, being exposed in the forest, but Mandor seemed unconcerned. He knew that the mare would protect them.

Just before dawn, the mare nudged Angel awake with her nose, nickering softly.

"Something's happening," whispered Mandor, staring intently towards the hideout.

Sure enough, through the gloom they could see Fraz emerge from behind the waterfall, and with a quick glance around, he scampered off, still unable to fly.

"Come on," said Angel, when he was out of sight.

"No!" said Mandor, as she went to go towards the hideout. "We follow Fraz."

"But Jack's on his own now."

"The mare will watch over him," he interrupted and set off after Fraz. "If we can find out what he's up to, we will have the advantage."

So they left the mare in the trees and followed Fraz's tracks in the snow, keeping far enough behind so they wouldn't be seen. As it was, Fraz kept stopping and checking behind to make sure he wasn't being followed. It didn't take Mandor long to figure out where he was going. "He's heading for Wystrazura," he said, not surprised.

Fraz stopped again at the entrance to Wystrazura, which was marked only by an unusually shaped tree. After once again checking the coast was clear, he scraped a claw on the bark and the trunk of the tree creaked apart to reveal a dark doorway and he disappeared inside.

"So he definitely is working for Jazzaar," said Angel. "Are we going to follow him inside?"

"Are you mad?" exclaimed Mandor. "Do you have any idea how many monsters there are in there? Have you forgotten what I told you?"

"I know, but we followed him all this way to find out what he's up to. We're not gonna find out out here, are we?"

"We can't go in." Mandor shook his head fearfully. "It's too dangerous. We'll have to go back and wait."

Angel sighed with frustration.

Although he had been successful in the task that Jazzaar had set for him, Fraz was still quivering with nervousness and fear as he made his way through to the centre of Wystrazura. The floor was littered with bones, and crawling over them, as well as the walls, were grotesque bugs that had been inside the tree all those years ago and had absorbed all the evil when Jazzaar was banished there. Faint screams could be heard from the people and creatures that Jazzaar had captured in his relentless quest for the Willowand. Nearer to the centre the air became thicker and hotter, as if it was the entrance to hell itself. Jazzaar was busy healing the Gragg's flank when Fraz found him.

"Well, well. My newest little disciple returns!" he announced. "What news?"

"The boy is alone, as you requested, Master," replied Fraz, his voice trembling with fear.

"And what of the girl?"

"She is gone. She is no threat to you."

"She is dead?" Jazzaar bellowed, jumping to his feet. His eyes glowed red as he glared at Fraz.

"No!" Fraz answered quickly. "No, Master; just gone, into the forest somewhere."

"Mmm…" Jazzaar sat back down, deep in thought. "She's not to be harmed. Maybe I can use her. How much does she know?"

Fraz managed a small smile of pride. "She knows nothing. She was asking questions about Maxus, but I told her nothing."

"So she is curious. She may have got information out of that cowardly skrift. She's not to be under-estimated. I have underestimated mortals before and look at me now." He paused to think again. "Proceed with the plan."

"What should I do about the girl?"

"Leave her; I'll deal with her myself."

★

Angel and Mandor returned to the mare to find her very nervous and disquieted. She told Mandor that though she hadn't actually seen or heard anything, she was sure that something had been close by. She may even have been seen, and insisted they move further back into the trees. Angel was fascinated, watching Mandor have this amazing conversation with a horse.

Fraz returned about an hour later. He knew Angel and Mandor had followed him – he was not the only one to leave tracks – but he was unconcerned. It was, after all, inevitable that they would find out eventually. All he had to do was to guard Jack so they couldn't get to him.

Both Angel and Mandor were not happy about retreating out of sight of the hideout, but they followed the mare. Her instinct had never let them down before. Plus, Mandor, as well as the mare, knew there would be a severe blizzard that day, and although they were perfectly well equipped to cope with such weather, Angel was not so lucky. They needed to find a place for her to shelter. They managed to find a hollow tree nearby, not unlike the one which Angel had sought refuge in on her first night in Equensia. Mandor set off to find some food and left Angel alone with the mare.

"Its OK," reassured Angel, sensing Jewel's sudden anxiety. "I promised I wouldn't ride you, remember?" She extended her hand to her. "Can we be friends?"

Once again, Jewel responded, remembering how good it had felt when Angel had petted her before. She sensed no danger. Maybe they could be friends after all.

Mandor returned with yet more oranges, just as the blizzard arrived. Angel retreated inside the tree, while Mandor and the mare stood close by.

The blizzard didn't last very long, but it had been so severe that Angel had to dig herself out of her tree. As the air cleared again, the mare took her turn to go and check the hideout. Both Angel and Mandor froze as Jewel's neigh of alarm rang out through the forest. They scrambled up to the edge of the trees.

"Oh, no," said Mandor as they watched the mare disappear behind the waterfall, and ploughed after her.

"Oh, no!" he said again.

The hideout had been completely trashed and Jack was gone. Jewel squealed, pawing the ground.

"The Gragg was here?" Mandor translated fearfully.

Angel's stomach churned. "So… Jack's dead?"

Mandor glanced around. "No. There's no blood. It's taken him."

"To Jazzaar?" she guessed.

Mandor didn't need to reply.

"Well, come on then! We've gotta get him back, before he ends up like Fraz!" Angel was beginning to panic. In the pit of her stomach she knew what his response would be, and she was right.

He shook his head, vigorously. "Oh, no. No way! I'm not going there!"

Angel went to put her hand reassuringly on his shoulder, but he shied away from her, saying, "No! I'm not going! Leave me alone!" And he ran off.

"Mandor!" Angel tried calling him back, but it was no good. She put her head in her hands. It was hopeless. She should never have let Fraz chase her away. Jewel nudged her gently, whinnying softly. Angel managed a forced smile and rubbed her ears. "I know, I've still got you." She sighed. "But even you have to admit we don't have much of a chance of getting him back on our own, right?"

Jewel nudged her again, harder, pushing her forwards.

Angel knew what she was trying to tell her. "It won't do any good. You heard him; he's not going to help us. And I don't think he'll change his mind either."

Another nudge.

"Alright, knock it off! We'll go after him. But I still say it's a waste of time!"

The mare trotted off in the lead, nose down, following Mandor's tracks. They found him cowering up a tree.

"Come on down," coaxed Angel.

"No! I'm not going!"

"OK! You don't have to go. We'll work something else out. Just come down," she promised.

Mandor peeped down at her suspiciously from the canopy.

"Come on. We'll find another way. Let's go back to the hideout, get warm and figure out what we can do."

It did seem like a reasonable idea, so Mandor relented and returned to the hideout with Angel and Jewel.

"This 'Jazzaar'; he went through a lot of trouble to get his hands on Jack. He obviously doesn't want to kill him, so what does he want?" summarised Angel, tidying up the hideout.

"The same thing he's always wanted – the Willowand," answered Mandor.

"But Jack doesn't have it, does he?"

Mandor shook his head. "His father had it."

"But his father disappeared years ago. What makes him think Jack knows where he is?"

"I don't know, but as long as he thinks that, Jack will be relatively safe."

"So we've gotta get him out of there before Jazzaar realises he really doesn't know anything. As soon as he realises that, Jack will be worthless to him."

"I'm not going to Wystrazura," Mandor reminded Angel again.

"I know; I told you, you don't have to." Angel frowned, thinking hard. "We'll have to find the Willowand ourselves and bargain it for Jack."

"Bad idea," Mandor shook his head.

"Well, I don't hear you coming up with anything better!" defended Angel, becoming rather desperate.

"If we had the Willowand, Jazzaar would just kill Jack and come after us."

Suddenly, the mare gave a snort of warning.

"Quiet!" translated Mandor, "Danger!" He crept to the edge of the waterfall. "It's Fraz," he whispered, "coming this way."

Without thinking, Angel picked up the spear off the floor and sped outside, hoping to take him by surprise. She succeeded. Fraz was shocked to see this previously pathetic, frightened, even shy little girl running towards him with a spear poised. He closed his eyes tightly in preparation as Angel literally pinned him to a tree stump by his wing. "Aaow!" he yelled.

"Where is he?" ordered Angel angrily.

"Who are *you*?" Fraz was still bewildered. He couldn't believe it was the same girl.

But Angel was thoroughly enraged and was quite prepared to kill him.

Fraz strained to try and free himself, but Angel held the spear firmly in place.

"Where's Jack?" she demanded again.

"He's safe. And alive. For now. Let me go!"

"Where?"

"Wystrazura!" Fraz yelled in submission and agony, and Angel let him free. "And if you want to see him again, you're to bring the Willowand to Jazzaar in one week."

"Or else what?"

"What do you think?"

"He's not going to kill him."

"Oh, really?" Fraz sniggered. "That shows you how little you know."

"Wait. How are we supposed to find the Willowand without Jack?" asked Mandor, appearing behind them.

"I'm just the messenger. You've got one week." And with that, Fraz scurried away.

"We shouldn't have let him go," said Angel regretfully. "We could have kept him here and maybe we could have traded him for Jack."

"Do you think Fraz is more important to Jazzaar than Jack?"

"Well, at least we could have forced some information out of him."

"Experienced in the arts of torture, are you? We know his plans now anyway. He plans to kill Jack, unless we get him the Willowand in one week."

"Hey, I thought you said that was a bad idea," Angel pointed out.

"Well, we don't have much of a choice, do we?" Mandor admitted, as they reached the hideout again. He glanced up at the mare, who nickered quietly. "Sit down," he said to Angel.

"Why? We don't have time."

"You're gonna need to sit down to hear this," Mandor insisted, and as Angel obeyed, he continued. "It's time you knew the truth."

Home

Home

Back at Wystrazura, Jazzaar was celebrating the best way he knew how. He had successfully captured and caged the son of Maxus. Surely that would force his old enemy out of hiding, and when he, the mighty, powerful Jazzaar, had possession of the Willowand he would be free; and no one would have the power to stop him taking over and ruling this land and all its occupants. Success was so close he could taste it! He even began preparing plans to rebuild his palace – a symbol of his supremacy. He drew up a list of laws, which basically consisted of death to anyone who refused or was even opposed to kneeling in front of him and making an oath of loyalty to him. "And you..." he stroked the heads of the two Graggs beside him, "my loyal subjects, will have all you desire."

Fraz had been stood in the corner, listening to all this, and felt he deserved something for his contribution to Jazzaar's rise to power. He immediately began to regret opening his mouth as Jazzaar glared at him.

"*You?*"

"Well... Master... I did assist in the capture, did I not? Surely that deserves something?"

"Mmm..." Jazzaar thought. "Yes. You're right. Come closer, Jabbott."

Fraz walked hopefully forward, though wisely he did not trust Jazzaar completely.

"You've done your job well."

Fraz was becoming very worried. Though his words were friendly, Jazzaar's tone certainly wasn't! "You... know I'm here to serve you," he stammered.

Jazzaar laughed at Fraz's anguish. "Well, that's nice to know; but you see, I don't need you any more."

Fraz swallowed hard as the two Graggs slowly circled around and stood behind him. "Please, Master..." he begged.

"Relax!" sniggered Jazzaar. "It's not as if I'm going to kill you or anything!"

Fraz breathed a sigh of relief.

"Take him below," he ordered the Graggs and they began driving Fraz in the direction of the dungeons.

"No! Wait!" objected Fraz. "If it wasn't for me, you would never have gotten this far!"

"I've let you live," shouted Jazzaar furiously, "is that not enough? I should have you sacrificed for all the trouble you've caused me in the past!"

One of the Graggs snapped viciously at Fraz, and he was forced to go with them.

★

At the hideout, Mandor rebuilt the fire and the mare stood guard at the entrance. Once again, Angel was kept in suspense for an agonisingly long time. At last, Mandor settled down and breathed a sigh of preparation. "I really don't think you're ready to hear this..." he paused, uncertain.

"Just tell me!" Angel was getting impatient.

"OK; how far back can you remember?"

She frowned. "What?"

"Just think back as far as you can. What's you're first memory?"

"What's this got to do with anything?"

Mandor sighed. "Do you remember your mother?"

Angel stood up, confused and frustrated. "This is getting us nowhere! We have to get out there and find this Willowand. Jack's depending on us!"

"He's depending on you."

Angel's frown grew deeper.

"You have the Willowand."

"What are you talking about? I haven't got a Willowand! I don't even know what a Willowand looks like!"

"Think. Think back."

Angel thought, then shook her head. "I've never seen it. How would I?"

"The morning Jack's father, Maxus, disappeared he wasn't alone. Jack had a twin – a sister. He took her with him."

"Why?"

"He would have taken Jack too, but he was injured. Fraz insisted on staying behind to look after him.

"What happened to Jack's sister?"

Mandor paused. "She disappeared too." There was another long silence until Angel took the hint. Her puzzled expression was replaced by one of shock and disbelief.

Mandor continued. "Don't you see? It's you!"

"Don't be ridiculous!" denied Angel.

"It's true."

"It doesn't make sense," she persisted, refusing to accept it. "If it was true, why did you say I was a monster when you first met me?"

"Because I didn't know back then. It's only since I've spoken to Jewel that I realised who you are. I told you, she goes to your land frequently. She has from the beginning. She's watched you grow up."

"So let me get this straight: if I believe what you're saying, then Jack is my brother, and my dad is some sort of lost warrior? Is that right?"

Mandor nodded. "I'm sorry. I know it's a shock."

"A shock?" Angel laughed in disbelief. "It's stupid! My dad is a rancher, not a warrior!"

"I wouldn't be telling you if circumstances were different, but you're the only one who can retrieve the Willowand. We need you to go back and bring it back here."

"Go back? How? If I knew how to get back home, do you think I would be here?"

"Jewel will take you."

"Jewel?"

"She's the only one who can make the journey. You'll have to ride her." Angel's heart leapt. "It's the only way back. I have spoken to her and she has agreed," Mandor went on. "You must ride her back to your own land and bring Maxus and the Willowand back here so he can finish what he started fourteen years ago and save his son; your brother." Mandor knew Angel's head was full of questions. "You must

110

hurry. We only have one week." He shooed her towards the entrance. "It will be quicker for you to ride her from here."

Angel didn't need telling twice, and grabbing a handful of the silky mane, she vaulted up onto the mare's back. The mare snorted briefly with discomfort, but didn't bolt. "Aren't you coming?" she looked around at Mandor.

"No, I can't. I'll wait here. Please hurry."

They set off at a gallop, dodging in and out of the trees. All Angel could do was hold on; the twigs and branches whipping her face as the mare forced her way quickly through the sometimes dense forest. They slowed down as they approached the pool.

The mare walked gingerly through the knee-deep water and stopped as she reached the other side and pawed at the water, neighing quietly. A wall of rock stretched up about sixty feet, the surface of which was covered with water like a sheet of glass. The mare stretched forward and nervously touched the rock with her nose. Angel gasped in amazement as the wall suddenly became transparent. She could see the mouth of the cave, her cave! And there seemed to be only a sheet of water between them. She eagerly and fairly desperately nudged Jewel forward, but the mare ignored her and just stood and looked, as if waiting for an invisible sign to say it was safe to go through.

"Come on!" Angel whispered through her teeth. Then, much to Angel's relief, the mare took a quick glance around and stepped through. Angel closed her eyes, preparing to be covered with the water, but they remained surprisingly dry as they got to the other side.

It felt good to be back in familiar territory. The mare strode faultlessly up the rocky slope and trotted purposefully along the trail. Angel's feeling of pride in how she must look riding Jewel was hampered by her concern for Jack, and confusion and disbelief that her father could have kept such a secret from her for so long. The mare paused briefly at the edge of the last fringe of trees and Angel gasped with relief as she looked out at her house. Home! "Let's go!" Angel nudged the mare forward and they cantered down to the gate.

★

Angel's father was stood in her bedroom, gazing blankly out of the window where he had been constantly since her disappearance. His heart suddenly leapt into his throat and he blinked as he saw what looked like Angel riding across the field on a white horse. He sighed. Many times he had seen the same thing, but it had always been wishful thinking. His beloved daughter was lying in a snowy grave somewhere. He watched her jump down and run to the house.

"Dad!" she called.

That one word seemed to break the spell over him and he darted out of the room. They met on the stairs and he flung his arms around his daughter and squashed her to him, almost in tears.

Angel was already overcome with emotion and buried her head in Dad's chest, taking a deep breath and reacquainting herself with the musky scent of him that she'd missed so much.

"Oh, my Buttercup!" he whispered and kissed the top of her head. "I thought I'd lost you."

For the first time in her life, Angel was overjoyed to hear him call her "Buttercup". He could call her anything!

He suddenly took a step back and looked into her eyes. "What happened? Where were you?"

Angel studied him. Did he really not know? "Equensia." She continued to stare into his eyes to assess his reaction.

There was indeed a hint of recognition. "Where?"

He wasn't fooling her. "Why didn't you tell me? All this time. I have a brother. And he's in trouble."

Angel's father had forced himself to forget about Equensia, his earlier life, but the mention of it brought back every memory.

"Dad, I need the Willowand," said Angel after a long pause. "Where is it?"

That broke him out of his trance. "I don't have it."

"*What?* But you must have it!" Angel was devastated.

"Why do you want it?"

"Because this... Jazzaar has got Jack – your son – my brother! And we need the Willowand to get him back. Mandor says it's the only way."

"You'll just have to find another way."

Angel frowned. "He's your son!" she reminded him.

He didn't need reminding and walked over to a window. He was perhaps the only one who knew everything Jazzaar was capable of, and imitating his daughter would be a classic trick for him to try to get the Willowand; but he wasn't falling for it. "Come with me," he said suddenly and headed for the door.

Trustingly, Angel followed him to where the mare stood waiting. She whinnied excitedly in recognition. He turned to Angel. "Touch her," he ordered.

"What?"

"Just do it!"

So Angel reached up and stroked Jewel's neck and she responded by nuzzling her tenderly. "What's going on?" frowned Angel, as her father placed his hand over hers as she stroked the mare's neck.

He smiled. "That proves to me you are who you claim to be."

"Of course I'm me!" Angel thought he'd gone mad. "Who else would I be?"

"Trust me. OK, come on. We've got work to do." He led her back to the house and up to the attic, which Angel didn't even know existed. "I locked this up years ago," he explained, and coughed as over a decade of dust was sent spiralling into the air. "When your mother disappeared, I just wanted to put that place behind me."

"But what about Jack? Did you never regret leaving him behind?"

"Of course! Every day! I tried for months to go back for him; but I was never able to figure out how to open the doorway – you know – the cave. I was stuck. Until now," he smiled and opened a large box, which was hidden under a load of old horse blankets. Inside there was a crossbow, amongst other things. "Be careful with that!" he said sharply, as Angel went to lift it out of the box.

"Wow!" she exclaimed excitedly.

"It's not a toy," he went on, and paused as he found an old picture of his wife.

114

"What's this?" Angel found a ring of oddly shaped stones, like a necklace.

"Be careful!" panicked Dad again, snatching it off her.

"What is it?" she asked again.

"It's a Dubring. Watch," he replied, eagerly anticipating her reaction, and skimmed it across the room like a Frisbee. It imbedded itself in one of the beams, but instead of stopping there it continued to spin around, sawing through the wood before returning like a boomerang.

"Cool!" Angel grinned. "We could have done with one of those yesterday!"

Dad looked questioningly at her. "I think you should tell me what's been happening."

So Angel proceeded to tell him everything that had happened over the last few days.

"...And so we've got one week to get the Willowand to Jazzaar, or he's gonna kill Jack, and Mandor thinks he'll do it too!" she concluded.

"I don't doubt he will. But he'll still kill him if I do give it to him. Just to make a point. I'll have to get him out before the week's up, and Jazzaar knows it. I'll be walking into a trap, but I don't have a choice."

"How?"

He paused. "I don't know. And I haven't got a lot of time to think of something."

"What's all this 'I' talk? You've got me and Jewel to help you."

"Jewel?" he smiled. "I suppose it suits her. And you're not going anywhere!"

"I know you don't think you're leaving me behind!"

"Damn right I am! I've already lost a family, wife and probably a son to that... snake! I ain't gonna lose you too!"

"You won't!"

"I know I won't! That's why you're staying here! End of discussion!"

Angel's lip curled in a defiant sneer.

"It's no good giving me that look, you're *not* going. I mean it!"

"You're gonna need all the help you can get."

Although he knew she was right, he also knew he couldn't bear to take her with him and risk losing her again. But what if he got back to Equensia only to find he couldn't return? If he left Angel here, she would be alone. He had made that mistake before and didn't intend making the same one again; so eventually he relented. Angel was thrilled. Her father – Maxus – couldn't understand her joy and excitement at facing what he knew was almost certain death, but she was young and unaware of what might lie ahead.

At the bottom of the box lay the Willowand. Angel couldn't hide her disappointment. She was expecting a spectacular, perhaps golden, sparkly belt; but instead it looked like an old – very old – stirrup strap that was due to be thrown out.

"Be careful," Dad slowly handed it over to her.

"Yeah, I can see why! It would probably fall apart!"

"It's very powerful." Dad kept his voice almost at a whisper. "Put it on. It will protect you."

"Put it on? Are you kiddin'? I dread to think where this has been!"

"If you're coming with me, you're gonna have to wear it. You'll need protection."

"If I wear this I'll need protection, alright! Parasites spring to mind!" She paused. "Oh, alright! I'll wear it. Over my clothes." As she fastened the belt loosely around her waist, she felt a strange tingling sensation flow right through her, followed by a warm glow.

"Go and get some warm clothes. I'll meet you downstairs," said Dad.

When Angel came down, her father was waiting for her outside with Jewel. She hardly recognised him with various weapons hanging off his clothes. He looked like a walking artillery! "Dad?" she frowned.

He tipped his wide-brimmed hat and signalled to Jewel, saying, "Shall we go?" He gave her a leg up before vaulting carefully up behind her and they set off at a trot.

"Wait!" he suddenly shouted, and Jewel stopped outside the cave. "Before we go back there, I want you to promise me you'll do everything I tell you to; do we have a deal?"

"Dad, I've survived three days in there on my own. I don't think you need to worry."

"Just promise me!"

"OK! Jeez! I promise!" Angel rolled her eyes and they slowly walked into the cave.

★

Mandor had been pacing the hideout constantly like a stressed leopard ever since Angel had disappeared out of sight. His senses were alert to the slightest sound, so he soon detected the crunch, crunch, crunch of feet approaching. His first thoughts were of the mare returning, so he eagerly went over to the entrance to greet them, but froze as, instead of the slender beauty of the mare, he was confronted with the black, shaggy stench of the Gragg. His heart was thundering unevenly as he held his breath, too petrified to move back into the relative safety of the hideout. The Gragg hadn't seen him and just drank peacefully. But suddenly it detected his scent, and without lifting its mouth from the water, it stared towards him. Mandor felt every hair rise up on his back as the Gragg locked eyes with him. Immediately Mandor realised that in the hideout he was trapped – cornered in a dead end. His only chance was out in the open; but would he make it to the trees if he got past the Gragg? There was no choice.

As soon as the Gragg was in the water, before he could drive him back, Mandor darted out as fast as his stubby little legs would carry him. The Gragg lunged at him, but missed, and Mandor fled for his life towards the trees. He reached them just as the Gragg caught up, and scrambled up the trunk, clinging on with every ounce of strength as the Gragg jumped up and grabbed a chunk of his thick fur in its teeth, ripping it out. His thick winter coat had saved him and he hauled himself out of reach. The Gragg shook the fur out of his mouth and ripped a piece of bark from the tree in frustration. Mandor peered fearfully through the branches panting. He was safe!

★

"Wait!" Maxus held up his hand and stared intently ahead. He slid silently off the mare's back. "Wait here," he whispered, and crept slowly into the trees.

Angel couldn't contain her curiosity and jumped down.

The mare whinnied quietly, pawing up the snow.

"Ssh!" whispered Angel, and she followed her father.

Maxus soon spotted the Gragg, still intimidating Mandor in the tree, trying to make him panic and fall. Keeping down-wind, Maxus circled around the Gragg in an attempt to bravely lead it away from Mandor, Angel and Jewel. He was just about to make his presence known when Angel spotted Mandor in the tree. She didn't see the Gragg until it was too late. "Mandor!" she called.

Maxus stared, horrified, as the Gragg bounded towards his precious daughter. "Angel!" he yelled, reaching for his Dubring, not really trusting himself to throw it and hit the Gragg and not Angel. He hesitated.

The Gragg skidded to a halt as it got to Angel. She whimpered as it sniffed her curiously and she screwed her face up in disgust as it snorted in her face. Its breath was positively toxic! She squealed in horror as it was literally sawed in half by the Dubring. Her eyes followed the blood-covered weapon as it returned to Maxus, and she swallowed hard as he glared at her.

"That does it! You're going home right now!" He was furious. Angel had never seen him so angry.

Mandor followed Maxus and studied Angel suspiciously, obviously completely baffled as to why she was still alive and not in the Gragg's stomach.

"It must be the Willowand," she explained in response to Mandor's suspicious expression.

"Come on." Maxus took her arm and forcefully led her back towards where he had left the mare. "You promised me!" he scolded on the way.

"I'm sorry."

"Well, I'm afraid 'sorry' doesn't cut it here! You promised me you'd do as you were told. If you can't stick to that, then we're all dead before we even start!"

"I won't do it again."

He looked at her hopelessly.

"Honestly!" she insisted.

Maxus knew he couldn't realistically send Angel home. He also knew her curiosity would get the better of her every time. He knew because he had been exactly the same at her age. He had two choices: he could either literally tie her down when danger threatened; or he could attempt to teach her at least some of what he knew about self-defence and staying alive. He eventually decided on the latter. "We'll make camp here," he announced as they approached the mare.

"What about the hideout?" suggested Angel.

"It's no longer safe. Jazzaar would expect us to shelter there. There's no reason to make things easier for him." He turned to Mandor. "Go and get some firewood."

Mandor waddled off.

"Get some rest," Maxus advised Angel. "We start your training tomorrow."

"Training?" frowned Angel.

"Do as you're told," he warned.

The sun had barely set and Angel was not in the least bit tired. "Why not start straight away?"

Maxus answered with a look.

"OK," Angel submitted, and sat down next to him, snuggling down into his shoulder. "Dad?" she said softly, without lifting her head.

He sighed. "Yes?"

"I'm sorry about Fraz." She knew the news of his faithful pet's death and resurrection to the dark side had hurt him deeply.

He sighed again sadly. "Get some sleep." And, as Angel gradually fell asleep, he silently and meticulously thought over the task that lay ahead of him.

Mandor returned not long afterwards and set about building the fire. He could tell Maxus was troubled; he had every reason to be. The flames soon began to dance in the air and Mandor settled down opposite him. Maxus looked completely lost in his thoughts and they sat for a while in silence. Mandor was becoming hypnotised by the flames and jumped, startled, as Maxus forcefully threw a twig into the fire, sending the embers and sparks shooting and spiralling into the air. "Things really have gotten bad, haven't they?" He sounded depressed.

"It could be a lot worse," Mandor tried to cheer him up. "You're still alive. And you still have Angel."

Maxus shook his head. "I shouldn't have brought her. I'm just gonna end up losing her."

"No you're not. If it was a mistake to bring her, she's still your daughter. Surely that's got to stand for something? And she couldn't have hoped for a better teacher."

Maxus smiled gratefully.

"It's really good to have you back," Mandor concluded.

Maxus had forgotten how much he had missed the little skrift. What he lacked in physical courage he made up for in wisdom and the ability to boost his morale. "It's good to be back."

"Really?"

"Sure. Though I do wish I could have saved Fraz."

"There may be a way. You have the Willowand. It has the power to heal. Maybe it can break the spell Jazzaar has over him."

"Maybe. But will he ever be able to trust me again?"

"He was always loyal to you, you know that. All you would have to do is say the word and he'd follow you again."

"I'm not so sure. From what Angel tells me, he blames me for all this. Maybe he's right."

"He's stubborn, he always has been. But he'd come round. Trust me."

Maxus smiled again. "We'll get him back."

"That's more like the Maxus I remember!"

"Well, this Maxus may be out of practice, but I'm always up for a challenge! Now get some sleep. Jewel will warn us of any danger."

Maxus didn't sleep much that night. As soon as Jazzaar found out about the Gragg he would know he had returned and would once again increase his efforts to capture and kill him. He didn't have a lot of time to prepare; and he was not as young as he used to be. Was he still up to it? It wouldn't be long before he would find out.

Training

Training

he moon waned; the sun rose and Maxus had barely blinked. He breathed a deep sigh as Angel lifted her head and sat up straight, stretching and yawning.

"Are you ready to learn how to be a warrior?" he asked.

Angel laughed, then realised he was serious. "Er…I don't know. What do you think?"

"I think we don't have a choice." Maxus got to his feet. Angel grinned enthusiastically and reached for the Dubring, saying, "Can I learn this first?"

"No!" he swiftly snatched it off her.

Her disappointment was obvious.

"Defence before attack." Maxus picked up a long, fairly straight stick off the floor and threw it to her. (Mandor quickly moved a safe distance away!) "You may get caught off guard without any of these elaborate weapons. I'm gonna teach you to use what's around you."

Angel sighed, feeling deflated. Sticks were boring! She wanted to use the Dubring and the crossbow. That was the exciting stuff!

Maxus picked up another similar stick. "Now; defend yourself." And before she knew what was happening, Maxus had disarmed her by whacking her knuckles with his stick, forcing her to drop hers.

"Aaow!" Angel clutched her hand. The pain brought tears to her eyes. Not only the pain, but also the fact that it was her father inflicting it.

"Pick it up," he said, fairly sternly.

Angel understandably hesitated.

"Don't grip so hard. Be prepared. Now, try again." Maxus had now given Angel a reason to defend herself. If she didn't she would get hurt, as in a real situation. It was the best and quickest way, though difficult for him. He had to force himself not to show sympathy and went at her again. He felt proud to see her react quicker, though still get her knuckles rapped. This time she didn't drop her stick, or call out. She sucked her teeth briefly and glared at him.

"Good!" he smiled. "Never show weakness or pain to an opponent. It gives them the advantage. Again!"

This time, when he came at her, Angel tried attacking back, and ended up having her legs swept from under her and landed on her back with a thud.

Maxus pinned her to the floor by pressing the end of his stick on her chest. "Defence before attack," he reminded and allowed her to get up.

"But how?" blurted Angel in frustration. "How do I defend myself without attacking?"

"I'll show you. Mandor!" he called.

The Skrift peeped out from behind a tree.

"Come over here and help me with this!"

Mandor shook his head vigorously.

"Come on! You know I won't hurt you!"

Mandor stayed put.

"I want *you* to attack *me*!" Maxus explained.

"Me attack you?" Mandor called back. "That's the first rule of defence: never overestimate yourself. No way!"

Maxus sighed. What else could he expect from a skrift? "We don't have time for this, Mandor. You have my word that I won't touch you, OK? Is the word of Maxus not enough?"

He still hesitated.

"Obviously not," he mumbled to himself, and turned back to Angel. "OK; you attack me. But don't concentrate on your attack. Focus on my defence, right?"

Angel nodded and obeyed the best she could. She was a quick learner and by the end of the session she was getting good at defending herself with her stick. Maxus was able to keep up his attacks for longer before catching her out.

Mandor kept his distance until the lesson had finished. Angel, though completely by accident, had managed to give her father a very painful whack on his face. His cheek had already swollen up and was turning red. She was very apologetic, but Maxus had praised her for it. Not many people could manage what she had, and he was proud of her for giving him a black eye!

As the days wore on, Angel's training intensified. Maxus taught her to make a particularly lethal slingshot using the bark from the peapor tree, and poison darts could be made using the hard wood of the lambin bush mixed with mashed nettle leaves and the droppings of a Jip – a small, carnivorous rodent that lived in the dense undergrowth. She even had a brief chance to practice with the Dubring. Maxus taught her how to hold and throw it; and, most importantly, how to catch it again so she didn't slice her hand off! However, Maxus still didn't think she'd learnt enough. And with each day the deadline was drawing nearer, though Maxus didn't believe for a minute that Jazzaar would stick to the deal.

Sure enough, as soon as Jazzaar heard that Maxus had returned he gathered his last remaining Gragg to him, and outstretched his arms once more. "*Inflectandar vicissitranzar!*" he chanted, and chuckled. "Perfect! Now go. And don't fail me!"

Maxus picked up his crossbow. "You wait here," he said to Angel. "We won't be long. Get a fire started."

"Can we do some more target practice after dinner?" she asked.

Maxus smiled. "Sure." He was really pleased by the way she had progressed, and turned to Mandor. "Let's go. I'm starving!" And they crept off quickly and quietly into the forest. Mandor was an excellent hunting companion. With his highly tuned senses, his tracking skills were second to none.

Angel had soon got a good fire burning and picked up the Dubring to inspect it again, smiling proudly to herself. "Boy, I can't wait to try this out for real!" she grinned up at the mare, who slowly backed off behind a tree, knowing Angel's aim still needed a lot of practice! Angel laughed at her, but then her heart leapt up into her throat when she heard twigs breaking and heavy panting as someone came stumbling clumsily through the trees. Angel jumped to her feet with the Dubring poised. "Who's there?" she called.

The mare pressed her ears back and reared up, squealing as a woman tripped and fell into their little clearing.

"Please!" she begged, cowering on her knees. "Don't hurt me. Please!"

Angel's eyes opened wide and she slowly lowered her aim. "*Mom?*"

The woman looked up with her panicked eyes and frowned. "Angel? Is that you?"

Angel was completely shell-shocked. She had only ever seen pictures of her mother, and here she was in front of her!

The mare reared up angrily as the woman slowly got to her feet.

"How can this be? All these years I thought you were dead." She slowly approached. "Oh, Angel, darling. I've missed you so much!" And they flung their arms around each other.

Angel was still beyond speech and as soon as her mother touched her, she began to sob uncontrollably. She didn't know if it was with relief, happiness or what – it was probably both. They stood embracing for a long while, as if it was an attempt to catch up on all the hugs they'd missed. "I can't believe you're here!" sobbed Angel.

"I know, my darling, neither can I. But I can't stay. There's something I have to do."

Angel could hardly see through her tears. "What? But... all this time..."

"I know. We've got a lot of catching up to do; but Jack is in danger."

"I know!" interrupted Angel. "Dad's here with me. We're gonna get him out. If you just wait a little while, he'll be back and we can all go together."

"You don't understand. There's no time. I know a way to get him out, but it has to be now. I can't wait."

"But it's too dangerous!"

Her mother sighed. "I know, but I've got to try."

"I'll come with you, then." Angel was desperate not to let her mother out of her sight now that she had found her. "I have the Willowand. It will protect us, right?"

"You have the Willowand?"

"Yes!" Angel lifted her coat to show her.

Her mother paused. "I suppose it would be useful. But I'm not going to take you with me. If your father came back and found you gone... I couldn't do that to him. No; I'll go alone. I'll be OK. Wait here for me. If I'm not back within four hours, promise me you'll go back to where you came from?"

"We have to get Jack out."

"If I'm not back within four hours it will mean I've failed, and there won't be a Jack to rescue. OK?"

Angel's stomach churned. "Here..." she quickly took off the Willowand and handed it to her. "Take this."

Her mother shook her head. "No. Maxus gave it to you. You should wear it."

"You said it would be useful. Just promise me you'll bring Jack back."

Her mother paused, then smiled and took the Willowand. "This will sure help. You could have just saved your brother's life," and with that she ran off into the trees again.

Angel watched her until she was out of sight before kneeling by the fire and breaking down again.

Maxus returned not long after. It had been another successful hunt. He was just about to brag when he noticed his daughter's tearstained face. He quickly knelt down to comfort her.

"It's Mom," she whimpered. "Mom was here."

Maxus frowned. "That's not possible."

"I know, but she was."

"Where is she now?"

"She says she knows how to get Jack out. I tried to get her to wait for you, but there wasn't time. She's gone to get him."

"On her own?"

"I know. I tried to tell her; really I did, but... even with the Willowand, it's still dangerous."

"The Willowand?" frowned Maxus suspiciously, hoping she hadn't done what he thought she had.

"Well, if it will increase her chances, I thought she could wear it..."

"Oh, no," Maxus stood up, running his hands through his hair, trying not to panic as his suspicions were confirmed. "You gave her the Willowand?"

"Well... yeah. She needed it."

He sighed. "Wait here." He picked up all of his weapons.

"She's coming back with Jack in a few hours," informed Angel.

"Jack will be dead in a few minutes!" scolded Maxus. "You've just handed over the Willowand to Jazzaar!"

"It's not productive to lay blame," said Mandor.

Maxus sighed, knowing he was right. "Just wait here."

"Maxus?" sang Mandor.

He turned back.

"She won't stay," he reminded him.

Maxus sighed again. "Well, come on then!"

They left Mandor with the mare and set off quickly for Wystrazura.

"I'm sorry," cried Angel again.

"No, I'm sorry," sighed Maxus. "There's no way you could have known what Jazzaar is capable of. It's my fault. I shouldn't have left you alone. Don't worry," he forced a reassuring smile. "We'll get it back."

They followed the woman's footprints all the way back to Wystrazura. "Oh, no," Maxus whispered to himself as he inspected the tree trunk.

"What?" whispered Angel, worried, not really knowing if she wanted to know the answer. "What is it?"

Maxus was thinking hard, and scanned the collage of footprints at the foot of the tree. He soon found the set that he didn't want to find. "He's out," he said, unable to hide the dread in his voice.

"Who?" Angel knew it was a stupid question, but the idea that Jazzaar was free was impossible to comprehend.

"Jazzaar," frowned Maxus, trying to think. "It must have been the extra power of the Willowand. He's out."

"Oh, no. What do we do?"

After thinking a while longer, he replied, "We follow him," and as they began to follow the tracks, Maxus was still trying to think what to do if and when they did catch up to Jazzaar. He tried to suppress the fear that was threatening to possess him. Fear would cloud his mind and render him helpless. He needed all his wits. Suddenly he stopped. Angel looked at him questioningly. He looked around at the position of the shadows on the ground and then looked up at the sun. "We've turned around," he said thoughtfully. "We're heading back."

"Back to Wystrazura?" frowned Angel, puzzled.

Maxus paused. "No," he suddenly realised. "Oh no. Mandor."

"What?"

Jazzaar had correctly and frighteningly predicted their every move and was planning to get to Mandor and the mare before they did.

"He's after Mandor!" Maxus said. "Follow me!" And they ran as fast as they could towards where they had left Mandor and Jewel. Sure enough, there was no sign of them.

"*Mandor!*" yelled Angel, but there was no reply.

Maxus immediately began to analyse the confusing muddle of footprints, hoping to find some sign to tell him they had escaped. But contrary to his hopes, Jazzaar had come too well prepared. They hadn't stood a chance. They had been surrounded and forced to go with Jazzaar, back towards Wystrazura.

"Poor Mandor," sympathised Angel. "He must be terrified!"

Maxus flopped hopelessly against a tree.

"We're gonna get them back, right?" prompted Angel.

"We can't just get them back, just like that. We have to have a plan. And it's gotta be a damn good one too! He's already as good as won. He is the most powerful sorcerer there is. He can just pick us off any time he likes. Do you understand? We have nothing to fight him with. These weapons won't have the slightest effect on him. The only chance we had was the Willowand. Now we don't even have that."

Angel began to cry again. "It's all my fault."

Maxus frowned sympathetically and opened his arms to her. "Come here," and as she accepted his invitation, he continued, "It's OK. It's not your fault. You didn't know. We'll get them back somehow." Maxus knew their only hope was finding a way of getting the Willowand back, but how? Now that Jazzaar had it, he was sure to guard it well. Not only that, but Jack and now Mandor and the beautiful mare were all expendable, so they had to be quick. Once again, he found himself having to repel despair. "Come on," he encouraged. "We'll think better on a full stomach."

So Angel set about gathering up the firewood that had been scattered all over the clearing in the struggle, while Maxus found and prepared the few large Jips he had managed to catch earlier. They looked anything but appetising as Maxus stabbed one with a stick and held it over the fire to cook; but Angel was so fed up of oranges that almost anything would have made a welcome change!

"Dad?" she munched, trying to imagine it as a leg of chicken. "I was wondering, why would Jazzaar go for Mandor? It doesn't make sense. I mean, I would have thought you would be more of a threat to him than Mandor. Why not just go for you – I mean us?"

Maxus frowned. She was right. Jazzaar had correctly predicted that they would follow him; so why not just set up a trap for them there, instead of going to all that trouble to lead them all over the forest? Unless this was it. Getting them to this clearing was the trap. There was no chance of cover as he glanced around himself. Sure enough, he spotted the first shadows flitting between the trees. Maxus jumped to his feet. It couldn't have been his imagination.

Angel was worried. "What? What is it?"

Maxus scanned the line of trees all around him. "You said you wanted target practice..." he said, his voice quivering slightly. "I think you're about to get a crash course."

Angel understood his meaning and quickly got to her feet, picking up the Dubring.

Maxus thought quickly. "No, hide it!" he whispered.

"But Dad!"

"Just do it. Now!"

Angel obeyed and slipped it under her coat before joining him in searching the forest. "Dad, I don't see anything."

"You will," he replied slowly.

"Let's hide."

Maxus grabbed her arm as she went to run off for cover. "It's too late for that."

"What do you mean?"

"We're already surrounded."

"But I don't see anything!"

He sighed, a little aggravated. He was trying to think and Angel wasn't helping.

"So we just... stand here, do we?" she went on, sarcastically. Then, all at once, she saw them – the circle of shadowy figures lined up all around the clearing where they were; just out of sight, barely visible. "Oh my God," she mumbled. "What do we do?"

Maxus had no idea. "Checkmate," he replied, eventually.

The silence was deafening, until Angel couldn't take this standoff any longer. "Well, come on, then!" she shouted suddenly. "What are you waiting for?"

"Angel!" hissed Maxus through his teeth.

She forced the crossbow into his hand. "Come on, Dad. Are you a warrior or what?"

Maxus dropped it onto the floor. "Only when there's a chance of success. There's too many. It would be suicide."

"Wise decision!" cackled Jazzaar's voice, causing them to feverishly search for him with their eyes.

"Well, I'm not going to just give up and go quietly!" Angel picked up the crossbow, took aim and fired. She knew the law of probability meant she was bound to hit one of them. She frowned as the arrow went straight through the figure and into the tree behind it, as if it was indeed just a shadow.

Jazzaar's chuckle rang out again. "You should teach your daughter some manners, Maxus."

"Show yourself, you ugly coward!" Angel was becoming catatonic.

Maxus put his hand on her shoulder in an attempt to calm her down. "Trust me," he whispered.

"If you don't show this child some discipline, then I'll have to!" Jazzaar's voice was angrier. "And you know what that means!"

"Angel, you'd better apologise."

"What?"

"Just do it!" he hissed.

"I'm sorry," she said, gritting her teeth, and mumbled under her breath, "I can't believe this!"

"Well, that's more like it!"

A sudden gust of strong wind forced them to shield their eyes and when they opened them again, Jazzaar was standing in front of them with his arms folded, just looking at them.

Maxus touched Angel's arm. He knew she was longing to lunge at him, and he knew such action would only worsen their situation.

Jazzaar smirked knowingly and slowly began circling them. "You've put on a few pounds," he observed.

"Well, you know. I've been away."

"He can still outfight you with one hand!" Angel retorted bitterly.

"Angel!" scolded Maxus.

"Really? One hand, eh? Maybe we could give it a try sometime."

"Ignore her. She's just a child. You may as well let her go. She is of no significance."

Angel frowned, hurt.

"Nice try," sniggered Jazzaar.

"Where's Jack?" said Angel, still trying to intimidate Jazzaar; a fruitless and dangerous aim.

"Jack?" Jazzaar pretended to think. "As you asked so nicely, I might just take you to him. I don't believe you've met my Shadow Warriors, have you?"

The Shadow Warriors stepped out of the trees and surrounded them.

Angel still refused to accept defeat and thought to herself, If these things are just shadows, then there is nothing stopping me running straight through them. She was wrong. As soon as she made contact with the darkness, her breath caught in her throat and she found herself gasping desperately for air.

Maxus quickly pulled her back and she fell to her knees, choking and coughing. He glared at Jazzaar as he laughed.

"That was good," Jazzaar laughed. "You know, I'm actually beginning to like you!" He giggled at Angel, still fighting for breath. "I may even change the name to the Shadow Angels!"

Maxus helped Angel to her feet and put his arm comfortingly around her.

Angel rested her head dejectedly in his shoulder as they allowed the Shadow Warriors to lead them off into the forest.

Capture and Escape

Capture and Escape

ngel could not fight back the tears and buried her head further into her father's shoulder in an attempt to hide them.

"Trust me," he whispered comfortingly. "We'll be OK."

"I wouldn't count on that!" snapped Jazzaar over his shoulder.

Angel had no idea how Jazzaar could have heard Maxus. After all, she had been as close as she could have been to her father and she had barely heard him! She didn't know that Jazzaar was capable of more than hearing the slightest whisper; he could also hear their thoughts – read their minds. It was an ability that had only recently returned to him and he planned to exploit it to its full potential. He smiled to himself. This Willowand was truly aweinspiring! He was invincible!

Maxus quickly silenced himself and tried to blank out his mind, realising Jazzaar's new capability, hoping he wasn't too late and praying that Jazzaar had not sensed his fear and insecurity.

After what seemed to be an agonisingly long trek, they reached Wystrazura. The enchanted tree had been uprooted. Jazzaar jumped up to stand on the fallen trunk of a once mighty tree. Angel and Maxus stood helplessly before him as he basked in his apparent victory.

"For too many years I have been imprisoned in this dungeon," he announced. "And now you must pay! Swear loyalty to me now, and I will make your deaths quick and relatively painless. Refuse and you will be subjected to a fate worse than death – a lifetime on the edge of hell, where I have spent the last fifteen years!"

Angel was petrified and couldn't have replied even if she had wanted to. Maxus just stood proudly and bravely, saying nothing.

Jazzaar laughed. "Fools!" he jeered. He knew Maxus would be too proud and stubborn to submit, and he had every intention of watching them all die very slowly. His eyes glowed red as the ground beneath them began to shake. The Shadow Warriors stepped back as the snow cracked and shuddered, disappearing into the ground as if through a giant sieve. They tried to keep their footing, but Angel slipped. The forest floor opened up and she screamed, scrambling desperately as she slid helplessly towards the hole.

Maxus made a grab for her hand, but he had begun to slip too, having no choice but to go with it. Thanks to his reflexes, he managed to hook his fingers over one of the roots that formed the intertwined web of the forest floor just a few inches from the top.

"Dad!" screamed Angel, feeling his hold beginning to fail.

"Hold on!" he called back, straining to hold Angel in one hand and the root in the other. Their predicament worsened as the hole began to close up above them.

whispered, and breathed a sigh of relief as she began to come around.

"Dad?" said a voice suddenly.

Maxus looked up swiftly and squinted, trying to make out the figure in the shadows. He slowly rose to his feet as Jack stepped into the light. "Jack?" he frowned, suspecting another trick.

Jack also hesitated. After all, for most of his life he had believed his father to be dead.

However, they didn't hesitate for long. "My son," said Maxus emotionally, hugging him tightly.

Jack flinched; after all, his ribs still hurt.

Then came the evil cackle that made them all sick to their stomachs. Mandor tried frantically to dig himself under a rock as Jazzaar appeared in front of them, laughing. "Very touching!" he jeered.

Angel scrambled to her feet and, without thinking, she took the Dubring out of her coat and threw it at him.

Jazzaar staggered playfully as the Dubring went straight through his hologram and began to saw through the wall of their dungeon until Maxus held out his arm, calling it back to him. "Nice," he complimented, still with the jeering tone. "Pity it does you no good where you are."

"What do you want?" asked Maxus. "You've got the Willowand; what do you want with us?"

Jazzaar sniggered again. "Yes, I have, haven't I."

"What do you want with us?" Maxus repeated,

ed. "I guess you can know. You will be anyone who defies me. You see, there may be a few small, insignificant forms of life out there that are getting ideas about trying to overthrow me. It's funny, I know, but I need a deterrent, and congratulations! You're elected! Because believe it or not, I am not a monster."

"Hmph!" retorted Mandor from behind his rock.

"I don't want to destroy anything unnecessarily," Jazzaar explained. "So I would appreciate it if you would please stay alive long enough until everyone has got the message."

"We'll never do anything to help you!" snapped Angel.

"Angel," warned Maxus. Her big mouth was going to get them into trouble again!

"Gee, that's a shame. Well, I'll be sure to tell them all who it is that's responsible for their deaths! Are you sure you want that on your conscience?"

Maxus glared at Angel, and she forced herself not to react. "Do you really think you can keep us here?" he hinted.

"Do you really think you can escape?" Jazzaar sniggered.

"Well, we did it before."

"Yes, but at what price? Your beloved wife! Who will it be this time? Your son? Or your daughter?" he faded away, laughing.

Maxus sighed, partly with relief and partly with the realisation that Jazzaar was right; he had lost his wife in the last escape, but that would just make him more careful this time around.

★

The mare's beautiful snow-white coat was streaked grey with sweat as she fought herself to exhaustion. Her perfect, neat hooves were cracked and chipped from scraping and slashing at the chains that bound her, and blood trailed from behind her ears and down her cheeks when she strained all her weight against the cruel spiked bridle. Her legs trembled and gave way beneath her, but fear forced her back onto her feet, her flanks heaving with deep, shattering breaths, as the impregnable ring of Shadow Warriors stepped to the side and Jazzaar approached her. Even he, the mighty Jazzaar, was in awe of her. She was the essence of spirit. Even as exhausted as she was, she reared up and lashed out at him, but he was, frustratingly, just out of reach. Then suddenly something was biting into her back and she swung around. The Gragg's teeth ripped her side and Jazzaar yelled furiously. With a flick of his wrist, he sent the Gragg crashing against the wall. The mare stood, shaking for a while, before collapsing again. She felt the immense evil generating from him as he touched her neck, but she was too exhausted to do anything to repel him.

"You will get used to your new home," he said, softly, maybe even with a hint of sympathy and understanding. "You are mine. Never forget that. There is no escape. You will help me regain the power that was lost to me, then you will die; I am powerless to stop that. I made you, and now I must break you. It is the way it has to be." He slowly backed away and the Shadow Warriors closed the circle once more.

The mare shuddered and fell into a restless sleep.

★

Angel began to examine the walls of their tomb, not really knowing what she was looking for but feeling a desperate urge to do something.

"It's a waste of time," said Jack. "We've been all over. There's no way out."

"Maxus?" said a voice suddenly, coming from inside a hole in the wall of earth, and Fraz popped his head out.

Angel immediately grabbed him around his long thin neck and held him against the wall.

"Hey," he objected, choking. "What are you doing?"

"It's OK!" Jack jumped in, trying to peel Angel's clenched fist from around Fraz's throat.

"I ought to kill you!" snarled Angel angrily.

"No! No, he's a friend!" insisted Jack.

"Maxus, help me!" croaked Fraz, trying to free himself.

But Maxus had heard all the stories about his defection to Jazzaar, and he was suspicious.

"Please!" he begged.

"OK, let him explain," said Maxus to Angel. She reluctantly let him go, but blocked the hole so that he couldn't escape.

"I have news about Jewel."

Angel erupted again. "You're still Jazzaar's little messenger dragon!" she accused.

"No!" he snatched his wing back defensively. "I am *not* a dragon! And I am not Jazzaar's messenger either!"

"Oh, really?" sneered Angel sarcastically.

"It's true," said Jack.

147

"Oh, come on! How can you believe this? He betrayed you!"

"It wasn't his fault. He's trying to make up for it," Jack turned to Fraz. "Isn't that right?"

"By rights I should be dead. Jazzaar used me, and now he's making me live with the guilt. I wish he had killed me!"

"What news about Jewel?" asked Maxus.

"She's confined in a chamber not far from here. I heard Jazzaar say he plans to kill her. I don't know when, but knowing Jazzaar he's not going to wait. He mentioned something about regaining power from her."

"I don't believe this!" persisted Angel, shaking her head. "It's rubbish! When it comes down to it, it's a horse! Nothing more!"

Mandor cleared his throat uncomfortably. "Well, that's not exactly true." He backed off nervously as everyone turned to look questioningly at him.

"What do you mean?" asked Maxus, rather menacingly.

"If there's something you know and we don't, you should tell us," encouraged Jack.

Mandor continued to back away. "I'm… not sure I know how to."

"Come on, Mandor," said Angel, softly. "You can tell us; it's OK."

"Well… it's true that she may have picked up certain… abilities during the… transformation."

"What transformation?" questioned Maxus.

"The spell… to transform her into… the mare."

Maxus's heart suddenly came up into his throat and he swallowed hard. "Transform who into the mare?"

Mandor flinched at the question and tried to make himself as small as possible. "Sonia," he mumbled submissively.

Maxus jumped to his feet. "*What?*"

Jack sat in shock, and Angel sat in bewilderment. "Sonia?"

"She was your mother," reminded Maxus.

"She *is* your mother," corrected Mandor.

"But... my mother's dead," Angel thought out loud.

"Why did you never tell me?" Jack had tears in his eyes.

"Does she know?" asked Maxus suddenly.

Mandor nodded. "She's retained her memories. And I never said anything because she begged me not to. She thought it would be easier for you to believe and accept that she was dead. Besides, you didn't need to know."

Jack frowned furiously. "*I didn't need to know?* How can you say that? All my life I had a mother and I never knew! How can you say I didn't need to know?"

Angel was also crying.

Maxus turned to Fraz. "Do you think you could get to her?"

"Maybe," he replied. "She's very well guarded."

"Could she not use these... powers she's got to escape?" suggested Jack.

Mandor shook his head.

"Why not?"

He paused. "Imagine your life as a burning candle. If she were to use her powers, it would be like

149

chopping her candle in half each time. It's not an option."

"We might not have any other options," Fraz pointed out.

Angel frowned. "That's my mother you're talking about!" she snapped. "And you're suggesting she just sacrifice herself?" She scoffed. "What more could we expect from a traitor!"

Fraz puffed himself up with a furious expression on his face.

"That's enough!" ordered Maxus. "We haven't got time to fight amongst ourselves! Fraz, go and see if you can assist Jewel—" he paused and corrected himself. "—Sonia, to escape."

"I can't believe you're leaving this to him!" objected Angel. "He's just as likely to go running to Jazzaar and tell him everything we know!"

"Well, what other choice do we have?"

"All we have to do is make this hole a little wider and Mandor could fit through," Angel suggested.

Mandor quickly hid behind a rock, shaking his head fearfully.

"At least he can talk to her," she went on.

"We don't have time," Maxus pointed out. "And Fraz has never let me down before."

"Except, of course, for getting Jack captured," Angel mumbled sulkily, and Maxus gave her a warning glare as Fraz scuttled off into the hole again.

"I tell you, letting him do this is a mistake!" warned Angel. "We should at least have a back-up plan."

"Well, I'm sorry but I'm having enough trouble thinking up a main plan!" Maxus snapped.

"Foolish, stubborn child!" mumbled Fraz and sneezed some particles of earth from up his snout, then froze with fear at the sound of Jazzaar's voice, coming from directly above him. The mare was being held some distance away, further along the tunnel, but Fraz paused to listen.

There was a deep, almost rumbling chant. Fraz could feel it in the earth under his claws and shuddered as the coldness travelled up his relatively short legs and along his body, making every hair stand on end. If only he could see what was happening. He thought for a while and then began scraping the soil away, constructing another vertical tunnel directly towards the sound. He soon reached the stone slabs that paved the floor of Jazzaar's newly constructed fortress. His horny nose heaved and strained to lift the slab just enough for him to see, but not enough for him to be seen. He spotted the Willowand, draped over a nearby boulder like a dead snake and held his breath. The Shadow Warriors stopped chanting as Jazzaar spoke. "It is time! Prepare the mare!"

The Shadow Warriors vaporised and Jazzaar left the room. Fraz's eyes fell once more on the Willowand and he paused. Time was quickly running out for the mare; and yet, here was the Willowand, apparently unguarded. With a second hesitation, Fraz gave another shove with his nose and flipped over the slab of stone. It landed with an enormous bang, made louder by the size and emptiness of the room, and Fraz flinched briefly, before making a scamper for it across the stone floor. He stopped a few feet away from the Willowand. Jazzaar would not be stupid enough to just leave it here without any form of security. He approached with caution, his eyes constantly fixed on the Willowand as it lay there, taunting him, inviting him to attempt to retrieve it and unleash some awful curse or a rampaging beast that Jazzaar had got locked away.

After another nervous look around to check the distance to his bolthole, Fraz stretched out his leg, hooking one of his long claws onto the buckle of the belt.

He paused. Nothing happened. Maybe – just maybe – Jazzaar was so preoccupied with the mare that he had forgotten to secure the Willowand. In the split second that it took for the thought to enter his head, Fraz became aware of the foolish mistake he had made. He felt before he heard one of the boulders to his left begin to move, joining up with others and starting to form a formidable mountain of rock. He didn't wait around for the terrifying form to complete itself, and, snatching the Willowand into his mouth, he fled, half running, and half flying (his wing was still not completely healed) towards the hole. He made it just in time. He couldn't leave without taking one last look.

The boulder monster stood about fifteen feet tall and rumbled. Fraz ducked as a fairly large stone was hurled at his head, and then scurried off back to Maxus and the others.

★

Angel was still sulking while Maxus, Jack and Mandor inspected the rough, uneven walls, not really expecting to find a way out. They all pounced on Fraz, relieved as he emerged.

"You got the Willowand!" praised Mandor enthusiastically.

"Hmph!" Angel folded her arms.

Fraz frowned briefly at her disapproval before turning back to Maxus to explain, "Jewel is running out of time. Jazzaar is with her now. I thought I would bring you the Willowand, while it was... unguarded."

"Good work," Maxus interrupted. He took the Willowand and closed his eyes, concentrating as hard as he could.

Angel gasped as the ground and walls began to vibrate.

"It's alright," reassured Jack, taking hold of Mandor's hand in case he decided to make a run for cover at the last moment.

The earth around them crumbled and Angel spluttered as the roof of their cavern split, showering them with soil and stones and roots, until, looking up, Angel could see the sky again.

Mandor shook the dirt out of his once white coat as the quaking stopped and Maxus fell to his knees.

"I can't," he rasped, panting. "I'm not strong enough."

"Let me try," Jack piped up, sensing an opportunity to prove himself to his father.

Maxus gazed up at the steep sides and sighed dejectedly. "It's no use."

Jack took the Willowand out of Maxus's hands. "Come on everyone. I can do this." He frowned as everyone just looked at him, knowing he was nowhere near ready to use the Willowand. "Come on! At least let me try!"

Maxus struggled, stumbling to his feet and shaking his head. "It would just wipe you out." He put his hand on his son's shoulder. I want you to try and climb out. Take Angel, Mandor and Fraz to the hideout and wait for me there. I'll try the Willowand again later and bring Sonia too."

"I'm not leaving you here," said Jack and Angel in unison.

"You have to. I'm not strong enough to come with you, not yet. And there's no time."

"That's why you need us," Angel pointed out. "Maybe if we combine our efforts... Just tell me what to do!" She was desperate.

It did seem to be their only realistic option. However, Maxus knew that even though the Willowand was of no real significance to someone like Jazzaar, it was still a power not to be underestimated or played with. It would be dangerous for anyone who didn't know how to use it properly; someone like Jack, or his beloved Angel. He couldn't bear for anything to happen to them. But Angel was, by her very nature, persistent and persuasive.

Jack sensed his father's hesitation. "It's just mind over matter," he said to Angel, and he stretched out the Willowand. "Everyone grab on."

Angel and Fraz quickly obeyed, but Mandor held back nervously.

"Come on, Mandor," encouraged Jack. "You want to get out of here, don't you? Trust me. You will be completely safe."

Mandor did trust him, but still had to fight against the strong instinct to cower behind the nearest rock, and as he took hold of the leather strap, Jack sighed in preparation, closing his eyes tightly. He felt immense pride as between them they summoned enough brainpower and the vibrations returned.

Maxus was rather impressed as the hole above their heads continued to widen. But suddenly, with a sickening crunch of ripping roots, a large crack branched out across the floor. "No!" he blurted. "Stop!" He grabbed the Willowand off them and, as if that was the only thing holding them up, they all collapsed.

Angel gasped, breathless, confused and frightened. She couldn't stand up! Every limb ached, yet she couldn't feel them.

Jack managed to regain his footing as Maxus knelt beside Angel.

"I can't get up! I'm paralysed!" she panicked, her eyes flooding with tears.

"No, you're not. You'll be alright," reassured Maxus, rubbing and slapping her legs.

She managed to get her hyperventilating under control as the feeling in her legs gradually returned.

Jack sighed. "It didn't work. We didn't make it." He stared up at the sky.

Maxus looked up and slowly rose to his feet. The extra corrosion seemed to have created several small platforms and ledges that might assist them in a climb. "You did fine," he assured Jack, trying to form a mental route up the wall.

Jack realised what Maxus was planning as he followed his stare. "Do you think we could make it?" he thought out loud.

"Hmm…" Maxus glanced back towards Angel; obviously not sure she could complete the climb. Maybe she could if they waited a while. But time was not on their side. Whatever they did, they had to do it now. He scanned the floor for anything he could use as a rope. The crack in the floor had exposed a few thick, flexible roots here and there. They looked like they could be joined. "Give me a hand with this," he said to Jack, and they tugged on one of the roots. It was very well imbedded, and it took a lot of puffing and blowing for them to free it. It was like a long snake, buried about six inches down, covering near enough the whole floor; more than enough to reach the forest floor, which was about thirty feet above them. "Stand back." Maxus reached for the Dubring, which effortlessly cut through the root. "Mandor," he beckoned, "do you think you could climb up there?"

"Up there? Oh no. I don't think so." He shook his head fearfully.

"That's freedom up there. If we stay down here; well, there's no telling what will happen to us." Maxus knew just how to get through to Mandor.

"Monsters?" he squeaked.

Maxus nodded. "Undoubtedly. Big grizzly ones."

Mandor needed no more persuasion than that, and he scrambled up onto the first ledge.

"You go up with him." Maxus put the root into Fraz's mouth. "Secure it to a tree or something when you get up there."

Fraz buried his long claws into Mandor's thick coat. Mandor barely noticed and continued with his vigorous, desperate climb.

Maxus smiled with anticipation as he watched them climb over the top and out of sight. Soon the root was sent back down to them, and Fraz's head appeared over the edge. "OK, come on up!"

Jack went first. Maxus helped Angel up onto his back and she wrapped her arms around his neck. With incredible effort they managed to heave themselves up. Maxus was exhausted, and partly strangled, by the time they got to the top. "I'm getting too old for this!" he panted, flopping onto his back. "I need to retire!"

There was no reaction from the others, so he turned to look at them. They were all gobsmacked. He followed their gaze.

"What the hell is that?" said Jack, his voice at a whisper, and Maxus sat up.

The Fortress

The Fortress

The towers stretched hundreds of feet into the air, spiralling like giant corkscrews towards heaven. They all sat with their mouths agape, but only Maxus knew what this really meant – Jazzaar's power was growing.

"Where did that come from?" marvelled Angel.

"The Black Fortress!" panicked Mandor, cowering behind Maxus's back.

"Do you think Jewel's in there?" wondered Jack.

Maxus knew she was, and without answering he stood up. "Stay here," he commanded.

But Angel ignored the sternness of his voice and followed. Jack hesitated briefly before joining them. After all, when Maxus, his father, had banished Jazzaar all those years ago, Jack was still a baby in arms. So neither he nor Angel had ever seen this fortress, with its shiny, black, impregnable walls.

"Where's the door?"

Maxus sighed with annoyance at his daughter's disobedience. "There is no 'door'."

"So how do we get in?"

"*You* don't get in!" Maxus paused. "Oh, what's the use?"

Angel smiled, triumphantly.

"Stay close to me," he went on. "And I mean close. This place will be full of booby traps. And touch nothing, OK?"

Angel nodded.

Maxus picked up a stone off the floor and Jack nervously took hold of his father's shoulder. "This is a bad mistake," Maxus thought out loud before hurling the stone at the wall.

Mandor fled for the trees as, with a deep rumble, the ground began to quake beneath them and they all fought to keep their footing. Angel skittishly searched the ground for something to hold on to in case the floor opened up to swallow her again, but this time the rumbling subsided safely. Angel breathed a sigh of relief.

"Come on," said Maxus, quietly and slowly. Cautiously, he led them the few feet towards the fortress. "No!" he grabbed Angel's arm as she reached out to touch the smooth surface. "Didn't I say touch *nothing*?"

"But it's just a wall," she objected.

"It is not 'just' a wall! You shouldn't even be here." He turned to face her, holding her arms firmly at her sides, demanding her attention. "I can't even hope for you to understand this, but I have been in here before. I barely made it out alive. You would never believe what lies in here and that was thirteen years ago! There's no telling what that warped mind of his has come up with since then…"

If Maxus was trying to scare Angel into staying outside, he was failing. All he had succeeded in doing was arousing that insatiable curiosity even more. With a worried sigh and a warning glare he turned back to the fortress. Angel and Jack watched in amazement as Maxus walked slowly towards the coal black walls and, without touching them, seemed to push them back, as if by the power of his hands alone.

For once in her life, Angel obeyed her father completely and followed him closely; so closely in fact, that she bumped into him when he stopped. She stepped back and found the wall behind her. They were in a narrow corridor, seemingly endless in both directions. "It doesn't look this big from the outside," she commented.

"It's an illusion," said Maxus in a calm but anxious voice, gazing around himself. The walls were imbedded with what looked like precious gems, some of which were glowing and providing the only light in the tunnel. He predicted his daughter's next foolish move: "Don't touch the walls. If so much as a hair off your head brushes against them, you will be imbedded in here forever. Follow me."

"Do you think you could lead us to Jewel?" Maxus turned to Fraz.

"Maybe," he replied, unsure. "I only saw the one room from above ground, but I think I can remember the general direction."

So, with arms fixed by their sides, they set off in single file, following the dusty Jabbott. It wasn't long before they encountered their first obstacle. The walls were becoming very uneven, with rocks jutting out in every direction. It was inevitable that one would eventually block their path. Being small, Fraz could jump through without a problem, but the others were stumped.

"Maybe you could just give me a leg up over it," suggested Angel. "It doesn't look that far; I could jump over it."

"Too dangerous," Maxus shook his head. "It'll be further than you think."

Jack took off his bark armour. "Here," he said. "Drape this over it. Then we can climb over without touching the rock."

Maxus paused. On its own a sheet of tree bark wouldn't be enough, but maybe, with the help of the Willowand, it could work... He handed the Willowand to Angel after climbing safely over himself, to test his theory, and soon they were all able to move on again.

★

The mare was being held close by, where she lay exhausted. She was not left in peace for very long and scrambled to her feet as Jazzaar entered the room. With strength that comes from fear, she fought against him once more but her efforts were in vain. She stood with legs trembling and breath rasping.

"Relax." Jazzaar's voice was deeply threatening. "Just as I have planned, your friends have arrived to find out they are too late. My little diversions will keep them busy long enough for my power to be regained; then you can reign with me on a throne of darkness forever." He chuckled. "And you will enjoy it."

The mare snorted and struck out at him again in defiance.

★

Back in the tunnel, spirits were high. They had successfully tackled the first of Jazzaar's "diversions" and they felt unbeatable; so much so that the first rumble, like thunder in a distant storm, went largely unnoticed. Fraz felt it under his claws, but said nothing until the thunder rolled again, considerably closer.

"What was that?" whispered Maxus sharply, and they all froze, hardly daring to breathe.

"Well, I don't really care, as long as it's not what it sounds like." Fraz's voice was considerably higher in pitch than usual, and quivering.

"What does it sound like?" asked Jack, dreading the answer.

The rumble that followed sent a shower of deadly dust off the walls, and they all jumped back to dodge it.

Fraz let out a pathetic, shivering whimper.

"I don't like the way you said that." Angel looked at him questioningly.

"Well... when I brought you the Willowand, it wasn't exactly unguarded as I made out."

"Great!" blurted Maxus sarcastically. "So, are you gonna let us in on the secret and tell us what is about to burst through this wall any minute?"

"It's just rocks, really."

"Not the wall, you stupid dragon!" snapped Angel, becoming very frightened.

Fraz glared at her. "I resent that!"

"Enough bickering!" Maxus demanded, as another shower of dust came floating down, this time with a few small stones too.

"Like I said, it's just rocks – boulders. Jazzaar must have put a spell on them or something."

"Oh, terrific!"

Just then, with another loud bang, a crack appeared in the wall, right beside them, like a shaft of lightning striking the ground. It wouldn't take long for whatever this thing was to get to them.

"Let's run!" suggested Angel, and she began running before waiting for agreement from the others.

"Remember, don't touch the walls!" called Maxus, as he and Jack followed.

But Angel saw, as she ran, more and more cracks and splits in the rock walls, and what was worse, these cracks were getting bigger and wider, until it began to crumble.

"Angel! Look out!" called Maxus. From behind her, he could see what was happening. The whole of the wall on the one side was going to fall, and if so much as a speck touched them that would be the end. He managed to grab her hand and saw the desperation and panic in her eyes as she swung around to look at him. "We have to jump," he said to both Angel and Jack, "as soon as it starts to fall and before it reaches us, OK?" Maxus knew this was the mother of all long shots, but it was all he could think of to do.

So they stood as far back as they could without touching the opposite wall. Fraz scampered up onto Maxus's shoulder, the safest place he could think of. They would have to get the timing exactly right for this to have the remotest chance of working. "As soon as I say, leap as high and as far as you can, OK?" Maxus instructed.

"I don't think I can do this." Angel was close to tears.

Maxus smiled at her. "Yes you can. You have to."

She sighed, her confidence draining out of her as she heard the continuous pounding and saw the wall slowly crumble with each blow, until she could see the room into which she would have to throw herself. Fear paralysed her briefly as she caught sight of the fifteen-foot pile of boulders mercilessly battering the walls with its gigantic stone arms.

"Now!" shouted Maxus, just as the wall collapsed, and they all dived through the legs of the monster. Maxus had been so preoccupied with getting them out of the tunnel he hadn't had a chance to figure out how to subdue and deal with this problem.

It stood for a few seconds, looking at them through eyes it didn't have. As if this mountain of rock wasn't dangerous enough, the boulders on the end of its arms were glowing red hot from the continuous pounding on the wall.

"He looks angry," commented Jack.

"How can you tell?" whispered Angel.

"It's a fair bet," said Maxus, discreetly reaching for the Dubring.

This monster was literally a mound of grey stone and didn't seem to have any vulnerable areas at all. Maxus had nowhere to aim, so just threw the Dubring and hoped for the best. All it seemed to do was make it angrier, and all that Maxus and the rest of them could do was dodge the blows that were aimed at them until they could think of something else. The solution was found quite by accident. Angel, while dodging another boulder, ran under the legs of the monster and set it off balance as it swung at her. Maxus then fell against it, while avoiding another large rock, and it was sent crashing to the floor, shattering into a thousand pieces.

They were all stunned for a few seconds, not really understanding that they had defeated it. They sat in shocked silence, the only sound being their pants of exhaustion.

Jack suddenly stood up. "We did it!" he laughed. "I can't believe we did it!"

Maxus was less ecstatic. "Come on," he said, standing up. "We've wasted enough time here." He turned to Fraz. "Which way to Jewel?"

Fraz found the slab he had moved earlier and soon worked out which way they should go, and they set off again.

★

They were getting closer, and Jazzaar knew it. There was no more time to waste. It was now or never. Even though he no longer possessed the Willowand, he still had power enough for this.

The mare had been tied down where she had collapsed, with thick, heavy chains. She could not even struggle as he approached her. Only her eyes could move and she watched him fearfully as he circled her.

"It is time," he whispered, and she shuddered, feeling his hand on her neck. Jazzaar sighed loudly, standing up straight, his arms outstretched, and the Shadow Warriors that surrounded them began chanting: "*Viredai potentia*"; the same deep, penetrating chant that Fraz had heard while burrowing towards this very room. Already Jazzaar could feel the power of the mare engulfing him like an invisible cloak and he gasped. *"Virendai victumagra!"* he whispered and closed his eyes tightly.

The mare could feel her spirit ebbing away and she was powerless to stop it. As Jazzaar revelled in the new surge of power pulsing through his veins, so the mare became less powerful, until she was a woman again, still beautiful, with her long, wavy, golden hair and piercing blue eyes, yet haggard and drained. Slowly, she heaved up her head and looked into the newly formed, extremely handsome face of Jazzaar; his eyes the only window which revealed his evil spirit; eyes which glazed black as they locked with hers. He gave an evil smirk as her brain yielded to the darkness.

Suddenly the large doors burst open, the bang echoing off the empty walls. Maxus, Angel and Jack stopped dead as Jazzaar turned to look at them and they stared in disbelief.

"This was meant to be a private party, but do come in. I have been expecting you," said Jazzaar menacingly, with a hint of sarcasm.

Maxus stretched his neck to look around him to where Sonia was still sat on the floor.

"Maxus!" she cried with relief.

"Mom!" called Angel, and ran to her. While they were embracing, Fraz noticed the tears of blood still rolling down Sonia's face.

"Angel! Get away from her!" he warned.

Jazzaar laughed as Sonia took a firm hold of Angel's arm, refusing to let go. "Yes, I'm afraid Mommy isn't

feeling quite herself today," he giggled to himself.
"She's decided to stay here and rule you. With me."

Maxus frowned furiously.

"Don't worry," whispered Fraz, "it's only temporary."

"Ah! The little Jabbott lives! I should have taken
care of you when I had the chance. Lucky for me, I
never make the same mistake twice." With a flick of his
wrist, Fraz was imprisoned in a metal cage. "I would
hate for you all to be misled by your little pet and his
misinformation. Thanks largely to herself, Sonia will
stay here forever, of her own choice. And to prove it,
in the morning, at dawn, she will be the one to execute
all of you, as an example to anyone else who defies
me." With another flick of his wrist, Maxus and Jack
were encaged too. "Don't feel bad," he sympathised,
obviously insincere. "You did your best, and just think
of all those lives your deaths will imminently save.
You'll be heroes!" He laughed and walked out,
followed closely by Sonia dragging Angel behind them.

"Damn!" cursed Maxus, thumping the bars.

"Dad?" said Jack, almost whispering.

Maxus sighed.

"What are we gonna do?"

"What can we do? It's curtains come dawn tomorrow."

"But that's tomorrow! It's hours away!"

"So what would you suggest?" Maxus didn't really
care. All he could think about was Sonia. She had been
dead; he could accept that. She had been transformed
into a horse; he could even accept that, but this?
Joining Jazzaar?

Fraz knew what his master was thinking. "It's not her," he said. "Jazzaar has possessed her mind, just as he did to me."

"I will not lose her to him again." Maxus vowed.

"But if what he says is true, we may already be too late. She has become the enemy."

Maxus turned to glare at Fraz. "That's what he wants us to think!" he snapped. But at the back of his mind, he knew the Jabbott was talking sense. Yet would he ever be able to see her as the enemy? In earlier years they had been an unbeatable team, producing two extraordinary children. No, he could never fight against her. There must be some way to free her. But in order to free her, he must first free himself.

★

"Let me go!" Angel struggled to escape her mother's painful hold on her arm as she was dragged through an archway constructed out of rock and into another room, which was just a dome of glass. Angel gazed up at the starlit sky and the trees – freedom. The floor was one giant mirror reflecting the sky, which was very disorientating. Stood against the glass were two golden thrones and in the centre of the room was a beautiful bed. Other than that, the room was empty.

Jazzaar turned to Sonia. "You have a lot to do tomorrow. Rest now." So Sonia let go of Angel's arm and lay on the bed, though her sleep was not natural. Her breathing was harsh and erratic.

Angel stared longingly out at the forest. The darkness promised to hide her. But it was an empty promise. It was an illusion that she could just run and disappear through the dense trees.

Jazzaar smirked knowingly at her deflation. Angel could feel his stare pulling at her, but she knew if she looked into his eyes he would pollute her mind as he had her mother's, so she turned away from him.

"You think you have the power to resist me?"

Angel scoffed.

"So did your little Jabbott friend."

Angel broke out into a sweat through fear and her heart came into her mouth. Her breath caught in her throat and she tried to stifle her terror as she felt him standing right behind her. She could see his reflection in the glass, like a ghost. She tensed up further as he leant forward to whisper in her ear, "So did your mother."

Angel cringed as her breath escaped as a mixture of a gasp and a sob, announcing her fear like a flare in the night sky.

"Join us," he hissed menacingly.

"In your dreams!" Angel tried to sound unaffected, but Jazzaar had seen the fear in her soul.

"I have the power to make my dreams come true. Yours too. I can give you abilities beyond your wildest dreams. You would be a fool to resist."

"Not as much of a fool as you! My dad will—"

"Your father dies at dawn!" Jazzaar interrupted her. He was losing patience. "And if you do not have a change of heart, then so shall you!" With a parting glare, he spun around and strode over to sit ceremoniously on one of the thrones. "Think about it."

Angel watched his reflection through the glass as, with a puff of black smoke, he disappeared. It had taken immense self-control for Angel not to panic. She had never been so terrified in her life. Her knees gave way and she sank to the floor. What was to become of her? Maybe it would be wise to join Jazzaar, but almost immediately she hated herself for even thinking it. She would rather die. Forcing herself back to her feet, she slowly walked over to where Sonia was still sleeping – if that is what it could be called. It was more like a state of limbo. Her mother was indeed gone, and Angel's eyes flooded with tears. "Mom?" she said softly, but there was no response.

Angel turned to look at the archway through which they had entered the room. With every step she took towards the dark hallway her determination grew. She would help her father and brother escape, and together they would defeat Jazzaar and make him eat his words! Her hands subconsciously grasped the Willowand, which she still wore secretly under her coat, suspecting a trap. She tried to focus her eyes on the end of the tunnel, for she was sure the walls were watching her. Quickening her pace, she was practically running when she got to the other end.

"Angel!" Maxus sighed with relief before returning to the task of freeing himself. Neither he nor Jack were having any success. Fraz, however, was making small progress. He had managed to move one of the slabs on the floor and was beginning to dig a burrow underneath the cage.

"Dad, we've gotta get you out!" Angel knelt down by the cage.

"No kiddin'!" replied Maxus. "Do you still have the Willowand?"

Angel quickly unbuckled it and handed it to him. Maxus looped the leather strap around one of the bars and pulled back as hard as he could. The power of the Willowand slowly and gradually disintegrated the metal until the bar snapped in two. They had to break three more of the bars before the gap was big enough for Maxus to squeeze through. After freeing Jack too, Maxus turned to Angel. "Where's Sonia?"

"She's in the next room, but Dad…"

"Then let's go." Maxus was not interested in anything except getting Sonia out. He had left her behind once before, thinking she was dead, and he had been wrong. He wasn't going to make the same mistake again. Fraz, who had managed to burrow out of his cage, ran to catch up as they all filed through the narrow corridor.

As they came to the opening, Maxus, who was leading, stopped. "Wait," he whispered.

Angel was still trying to prepare her father. "Dad, she's not the same person…"

"Quiet!" he demanded, refusing to listen. He forced the Willowand back into Angel's hands. "Put this back on." He slowly peeped around the edge of the wall into the room.

"But Dad…" persisted Angel.

"Maxus, listen to her!" said Fraz.

Maxus pulled a dagger out of his belt. "OK. We'll just go in and see. That's all. And if she has joined up with Jazzaar, then… then I'll kill her." He could hardly bring himself to say it, and there was no way he could actually do it. So he just entered the room, hoping it wouldn't come to it. He couldn't help but gaze briefly around the extraordinary dome with its mirrored floor as he slowly approached the bed, raising the dagger into the air just as a precaution. "Please," he prayed silently, "don't make me do this." Maxus paused, the jagged edge hovering. As he looked down on her, as she slept; she was his beautiful Sonia again.

Fraz scampered up onto his shoulder. "What are you waiting for?" he whispered, and as Maxus's eyes were drawn down to gaze at her again, he heard the same voice whispering in his ear, "Kill her."

He shook his head and the knife slowly lowered, ending up by his side. "I can't."

"You have to!" The voice was becoming more desperate. "This could be your only chance. Do it!"

But he couldn't and he stepped back.

"Er… Dad?" Angel nudged her father, signalling to where Jazzaar had appeared sitting on his throne again.

"Jazzaar!" said Fraz bitterly.

He sighed. "You are a spoilsport! I was enjoying that!" Jazzaar glared at Fraz, who suddenly disappeared in a ball of green flames. "That's better!"

"Fraz!" blurted Jack.

"I apologise about your little pet. But he was becoming a bore. I see you've found your lovely wife."

"What have you done to her?" Maxus glared at Jazzaar.

"Who, me? Nothing."

"Liar!" accused Angel.

Jazzaar turned swiftly to look at her, but she wisely avoided eye contact. "So I see you have made your choice." He stood up.

"Wait!" Maxus blurted, knowing Jazzaar was about to do something terrible.

But he already had Angel in his glare. "*Nectosolvo abkarin!*"

Angel froze, her whole body turning numb from the inside out; bones, then muscles, then her skin; and it petrified her. She was sure she even heard her own heart stop beating.

"Stop!" begged Maxus desperately, and to his horror he saw his daughter turn to dust and disappear, followed closely by Jack. He was alone, and collapsed to his knees in despair.

Jazzaar frowned at him. "What's happened to you?" He walked over to him, still frowning suspiciously. "Come on. Get up."

But he couldn't. His reason for living had just disintegrated before his eyes. He had nothing left to fight for.

"I have waited so long for this moment," Jazzaar went on with a hint of sadness. "And now I find myself wondering what it was all for. Maybe it would have been better if you had never returned. You're not the same man you were fifteen years ago. Maybe if you had realised that, you could have saved us all a lot of trouble. At least you would still have a daughter."

Maxus glared up at him. "Don't you *ever* talk about my daughter!"

Jazzaar grinned as he saw the rage on Maxus' face. "How does it feel, knowing you could have saved her?"

Maxus leapt to his feet in fury.

"That's more like it!" Jazzaar smiled, seemingly unaffected by Maxus's hands around his throat. "That's the warrior I remember!"

Maxus pushed himself away, quivering with anger, and Jazzaar laughed at his torment. Jazzaar took a quick glance at Sonia, summoning her to awake, and as she sat up, Jazzaar backed off to sit back down. "If I were you, I would arm yourself," he advised.

Sonia advanced towards Maxus slowly; her eyes were glazed, as if she were a robot.

"Sonia?" he said hopefully, backing away. But she was immune to his voice, which always used to calm her. He soon realised his worst fear: he would have to fight...

The Black Knight

The Black Knight

ngel didn't know how long she had been lying unconscious, but as her senses gradually returned to her she came to realise she was in a dark, damp cavern – and she wasn't alone. Her limbs were still not completely under her control, but she managed to scramble into the shadows. She didn't recognise this place as the Phantom Zone; a particularly unpleasant and depressing corner of Wystrazura, left to rot for almost fifteen years. The rustlings got louder until she saw the silhouette of a creature. Angel held her breath so as not to make the slightest sound; her curiosity hampered by not knowing whether or not the small, pixie-like creature was friend or foe. Stood upright it may have made three feet tall, though it got around mainly by an awkward-looking and rather comical stoop. Its legs were covered in a fine fur from the knee down, the colour of which was unrecognisable in the dark. From what she could make out, it was collecting some sort of plant. Angel flattened herself against the slimy rock of the wall as the strange little being bustled closer. The stench was almost unbearable and she had to hold her breath again, just to escape it. How could anything smell this bad? She had never smelt death, but imagined not even that could come close.

The animal's eyes, not unlike those of a sheep, seemed to pierce the darkness that concealed her, and it smiled and beckoned to her. "Come, come," it said, in a surprisingly soft voice, unfitting to its rugged appearance.

Inevitably Angel had to take a breath, and she could taste the putrid air in her throat like poison. She was unwilling to follow the creature, so it backed away to where Jack lay not far away. It was his helplessness which eventually brought her out of the shadows. "Hey," she said, trying to sound unafraid, "leave him alone."

It turned to face her again, and gasped as it spotted the Willowand under her coat. Angel quickly covered it up, and it slowly turned back to Jack, squatting down beside him, mumbling in what sounded like a strange language.

"Who are you?" asked Angel in the same tone.

There was no reply – only more mumbling.

"Come on! I know you can speak English! 'Come, come,' remember?"

"Hah! Come, come!" the creature seemed thrilled, excited, and grinned at her, revealing its six narrow, needle-like teeth, which looked grey in the gloom.

"Is that all you can say?" guessed Angel, frowning in puzzlement. "What are you?"

"Come, come," it grinned.

Angel knelt down beside Jack. He was still alive, though only just. She sighed. "My name's Angel, anyway. I don't suppose you can tell me where I am could you?"

She wasn't expecting a reply, so was shocked when she got one. "Bad place. Not stay here. Limfit friend to Angel. Must leave."

"Limfit? Is that your name?"

"Must leave!" he insisted.

"Believe me; I would love to, but how?"

Suddenly, the limfit seemed to panic for no reason.

"What?" said Angel, concerned.

He grabbed her arm tightly.

"Aaow! Stop it! You're hurting me!" she objected, but he dragged her into one of the few patches of light which littered the floor.

"Must be quiet!" he whispered. "The Black Knight. He hunts Limfit. Must be quiet!"

"What black knight?" Angel could see nothing, blinded by the spotlight in which they stood, but the terrified limfit was trembling with fear. This didn't seem the best place to try and hide. In fact it was a ridiculous place to hide, but no way could she make the stupid limfit understand that they were actually advertising their presence by standing where they were. But only the limfit knew that the Black Knight could not enter the light, and they were actually in the only place that was safe. It could only see in the dark, and provided they kept perfectly quiet, they may go undetected, even by the horse's exceptional sense of smell. But not while he was having to explain all of this to a stupid girl!

Eventually, Angel grasped the general idea; just in time, as she heard the rhythmic sound of a horse's hooves coming closer. It seemed impossible that they could pass so close and still not see them; so close that

Angel had to quickly move her arm out of the dark as they brushed past. She stared out into the blackness. "What about Jack?" she whispered. "We should move him into the light."

But the limfit grabbed her arm, forcing her to stay still.

Angel was terrified; her head was pounding as the sound of the Black Knight's searching continued. She felt helpless; especially for Jack. She had to do something, but what? She closed her eyes tightly as her headache got worse. She had never experienced a headache so intense before; it felt as if her head was being crushed in a vice; then something snapped in her mind. It was as if everything, all her past life in Equensia, as short as it had been, had become clear to her; and she was no longer afraid. She was the daughter of Maxus, and all of a sudden she knew exactly what she had to do. The limfit held its breath and watched her intently as she slowly unbuckled the Willowand from around her waist. "Danger!" it whispered, predicting what she was about to do.

"Don't be afraid," Angel whispered back, focusing her eyes on the shadow that was still moving around, searching for them. She looked over to where Jack was still laid about ten feet away. "Wake up," she thought silently, and jumped, startled, as he moved. What was happening to her? How was it she could do all this? She didn't know, but didn't pause for long. As soon as Jack began to move, she knew the Black Knight would spot him. Sure enough, she heard the hoofbeats as the horse galloped towards him. Angel moved as fast as she could in an attempt to get to Jack first. She jumped between them, holding the Willowand above her head just as the Black Knight swung his mighty sword at her. She flinched briefly as the Willowand snapped the sword in half, emitting a blinding light, and Angel closed her eyes and covered her ears as the light was followed by a deafening, ear-piercing screech. The Black Knight was destroyed. Angel, after replacing the remarkable Willowand back around her waist, swung around as she heard the snorting and saw the Knight's horse trotting through the darkness, completely disorientated without its rider. Jack watched her, baffled at the change in her as she set about catching the confused horse. It didn't take her long and she vaulted up onto its back, grabbing on to the long black mane. Jack frowned, suspicious, as she brought the magnificent horse to a standstill in front of him. "Come on," she said eventually.

"How did you know to do that?" he asked.

Angel thought for a while. "I don't know!" She sniggered. "I was good, wasn't I?"

Jack didn't reply; just continued to frown at her, suspiciously. She was good – too good. He couldn't help thinking there was something she wasn't telling him. There wasn't, of course. Angel was just as baffled as he was as to why she could do all this warrior stuff. She wasn't complaining, however. She liked the fact that she was a warrior; it made her feel invincible. "Maybe it's the Willowand helping us," she suggested after a while, feeling she had to explain herself. "Come on. Do you want to get out of here or not?"

Jack scrambled to his feet. Maybe his sister was bewitched with sorcery, but he wasn't about to be left behind in this place, and he jumped up behind her.

Angel looked down at the limfit and he bowed humbly in front of her.

"You are mighty warrior," he said. "Limfit thanks you."

"Come with us," she said.

But he shook his head. "This is Limfit's home."

"But it's horrible here..."

"Come on. He's happy here," said Jack. "This is where he belongs."

Angel sighed. "OK. Goodbye Limfit. Thank you."

"You're saying goodbye, but how do you plan on getting out of here?" Jack pointed out.

"The horse knows."

"How do you know that?"

Angel frowned. She had no idea; she just knew.

"What's going on? What's happening to you? How come you know all this stuff all of a sudden? And don't say it's the Willowand, 'cause you still wouldn't know all this."

Angel couldn't explain it. "I don't know. All I know is, we've gotta get out of here and help Dad. And I know the horse knows the way, so I'm going. Are you coming or not?"

Jack was still not satisfied, but he went with her.

The air became thicker and blacker the further they went, like being buried alive, and both Angel and Jack were finding it increasingly difficult to breath.

"Angel?" whispered Jack breathlessly. "Where are we going?"

"I don't know," she replied, becoming worried.

Suddenly, the horse stopped. Angel and Jack tensed up, preparing themselves for whatever was coming next. They could see absolutely nothing, and could only hang on as the horse took a few steps backwards.

"What's happening?" Jack whispered timidly.

Then, with a gigantic buck, the horse struck out with both of its hind legs, sending sparks flying off rock. It bucked, and bucked again, hitting the rock each time.

Angel's first thought was that it was trying to throw them off, and she gripped on to a larger chunk of mane. But as the horse turned around she could see small specks of light, briefly, before the large black horse rose up on its hind legs and began striking out again, this time with its forelegs. Each strike would chip away more rock, until there was a large enough gap for them to walk through.

The ground was very uneven, but the dark stallion didn't stumble once over the large boulders that littered the floor. They went a little further before Angel realised where they were. As they reached the top of a particularly large mound of rock, they came in sight of the fortress. It was night, and the tall towers looked even more frightening and intimidating in the dark; but they didn't stop to admire the view. Angel and Jack were ready as the horse reared up again to gain entrance, but as he struck out there was nothing there and he dropped back down onto all four feet, maybe a little confused, but Angel nudged him forward. They went back through the tunnel, being sure not to touch the walls, and came across the remains of the boulder monster before finding the room where Jazzaar had imprisoned them, and on towards the room where Angel last saw her father.

★

Maxus had been forced to fight the only woman he had ever loved. Still, he refused to do anything but defend himself against her attack; and all the while, he was trying to get through to her; trying to snap her out of the spell that Jazzaar had over her, until she collapsed with exhaustion. He searched her eyes, desperately trying to find an ounce of the Sonia he knew – his Sonia; but she had gone. All that was left was this cowering creature. Then suddenly a tear appeared in her eye; a glimmer of his beloved Sonia, fighting to emerge. "Please," she begged, "kill me."

"Yes, why not?" Jazzaar grinned evilly, as Maxus turned to glare at him. "Well, go on. Kill her again. You did it once before."

"You would love to believe that, wouldn't you?"

"Face it; we're the same."

"He's nothing like you!"

Jazzaar swung round to find Angel stood in the archway on a glistening black horse. How could she have survived?

She sat proudly, as both Jazzaar and Maxus stared at her in disbelief. "Dad? Are you OK?" she asked, as Jack jumped down and ran to stand at his father's side.

Maxus gasped with relief. His children were alive! How, he didn't know; but by some miracle they were stood there. His elation was matched equally by Jazzaar's dread. Almost immediately he realised something was different about Angel, and he saw his own doom in her face. This child should be dead; they both should. Then he spotted the Willowand around Angel's waist. "Give me the Willowand, child," he said, trying to hide his own nervousness.

The horse reared up once more. "You had better stay back," threatened Angel.

"Do you like my horse?" Jazzaar stroked the silky arched neck, as the horse stood, snorting. "A magnificent animal, don't you think?"

"Angel?" said Maxus nervously. "Come on down from there."

"Stay back," Angel warned again.

"Angel..." Maxus persisted.

"If this is your horse, how come he helped us get out of... that place you sent us?"

Jazzaar smirked, sneaking ever closer to the Willowand, inch by inch. "Did you like it there? How did you defeat the Black Knight?"

"It was easy!" she bragged. "Piece of cake!"

"Really?"

Angel jumped down away from Jazzaar. "Don't think I don't know what you're trying to do."

"And what's that?"

"Get your hands on this Willowand! You'll never get it!"

"Really?" Jazzaar smirked again, as Angel ran over to stand with her father and brother. He sighed. "Why not just give it up? We all know you don't stand a chance, and I'm... well, frankly I'm bored with fighting this. The outcome is inevitable. And let's face it, you have no idea how that Willowand works. It would be wasted in your hands."

"Try me."

"What did you say?" Jazzaar couldn't believe his ears.

"Angel…" warned Maxus.

"I said, 'Try me!' Give it your best shot!"

Jazzaar couldn't hold back the laughter. "You? Against me?"

Angel just glared at him.

"Angel, don't be stupid," said Maxus.

"Maybe we should let her try," said Jack.

Maxus looked at him in disbelief.

"You should see the stuff she did earlier. She was good!"

Jazzaar's amusement turned to anger. "Good? *Good?* You have no idea the harm I can inflict on you! How dare you even challenge me?"

Angel scoffed. "That's one hell of an ego you have there. Do you want to know what I think? I think you're scared. That's why you want the Willowand so much; because while I have it, I can challenge you, and I will defeat you."

"You can never defeat me."

Maxus was watching and listening, his mouth agape. "What's happened to her?" he whispered to Jack.

Jack shrugged his shoulders. "I don't know, but she destroyed that knight without a second thought."

Maxus thought for a while. He was torn between stopping his daughter from what was almost certain suicide and having the same blind faith that she seemed to have in herself.

But there was no time for him to make any decision. Angel slowly unbuckled the Willowand from around her waist again, as she sensed Jazzaar was about to attack.

"Now is your last chance to surrender," warned Jazzaar, and he glanced over to Maxus. "Don't be a fool. If you have any control over this child, then now is the time to use it before I send her back to the Phantom Zone; and believe me; this time she will not return."

"Dad," whispered Jack. "Do something."

"What happened to, 'Let her try'?"

Jack swallowed hard. He had as many concerns as Maxus did about Angel's new-found confidence and abilities.

"Wait!" Maxus blurted as Jazzaar outstretched his arms. "Angel! I will not lose you again!"

Angel turned to her father. "Dad, trust me! I'll be fine!"

That was the moment Jazzaar was waiting for. As soon as Angel's attention was diverted from him, he sent his spell: "*Coactufim parylac!*"

Angel was lifted up by an invisible force and thrown across the room against the glass of the dome. She couldn't breathe, as if something had her around the throat and was choking her.

Jazzaar grinned.

"Enough!" urged Maxus.

"Silence!" commanded Jazzaar. "You had your chance!" and he strutted over to where Angel lay, completely paralysed and fighting for breath. "Now do you surrender?"

Angel gripped onto the Willowand and slowly the effects of the spell began to disperse.

Jazzaar frowned as he saw her recovering and outstretched his arms again, but Angel was ready for him this time, and she unbuckled the Willowand. "*Coactio!*"

Angel held up the Willowand just as Jazzaar sent the spell, rebounding it. It was Jazzaar who was sent flying across the room by his own spell and Angel managed to stagger to her feet. She approached him slowly, still coughing. "Now do *you* surrender?"

Jazzaar looked up at her, and with incredible effort managed to force out a mocking laugh. "You can never defeat me," he said again.

"Really?" Angel coughed again. "Why would you say that?"

"Look into my eyes."

"You think I would fall for that?"

"You have the Willowand, don't you? Don't you trust it to protect you? Look into my eyes; what are you afraid of?"

"Angel, don't!" called Maxus and Jack together.

Angel paused. She had no intention of being possessed; but unknown to her, Jazzaar was planning something a lot more devastating than mere possession.

"Go ahead," Jazzaar encouraged as he struggled to his feet.

Angel turned away from him to avoid his stare.

"Don't you want to know where all your knowledge came from? Don't you want to know why Goliath over there let you ride him? Don't you see; you can never defeat me because I'm your father."

"You're a liar!" screamed Angel.

Maxus frowned furiously. "Angel, don't listen to him. He's trying to poison your mind."

Jazzaar turned swiftly towards him. "You know it's true. You've always known; and all this new ability proves it!" He turned back to Angel. "We were meant to rule together, you and me. That is why you're here." He smirked as he saw a tear trickle down her cheek. "I know you hate me now, but it's my blood in your veins, and not even I can change the truth." Angel's head lowered and Jazzaar gently but firmly grasped her shoulders and turned her to face Maxus. "You know what you have to do."

"Angel, no," Maxus knew as well as Angel did that Jazzaar meant for her to kill him.

She was confused. She knew instantly the spell to stop his heart beating, so maybe Jazzaar was right. Maybe she really was his daughter, but she was also, and more so, the daughter of Maxus.

"*Impetectium necojazztar*," she said, directing the spell straight at Jazzaar, who staggered backwards against the glass of the dome and sank to his knees, looking at her with a strange, even fearful expression on his face. As she watched him die, she looked into his eyes for the first time and saw her own reflection before they glazed over and he disappeared in a tornado of dust.

When he had gone, Angel collapsed with complete mental, physical, emotional and magical exhaustion. Jack and Maxus ran over to her and helped her to her feet again. She couldn't feel her legs; every muscle was shaking uncontrollably. "Dad?" she mumbled. Even speaking was enough to wear her out.

Maxus pressed her head into his shoulder. "Oh, Angel, you have no idea how happy I am to hear you say that!" He practically carried her over to one of the thrones and sat her down. "Rest now."

"Mom?" she looked over to where Sonia had collapsed. Now that Jazzaar was gone she was free of his sorcery, and she sat up, glancing down at herself, not believing she was human again after thirteen years. Sonia looked up to see Maxus, Jack and Angel and her eyes flooded with tears of relief. Maxus ran to her and helped her up. "Where the hell have you been? You sure took your time!" she said, and laughed the best she could. Angel looked at them; her mother and father, together again. It was like a dream. They were a family again.

"Let's get out of here," said Maxus, and he lifted Angel and Sonia up onto Goliath's back and they made their way out of the fortress.

★

The forest had taken on a whole new shape as they left the ruins of the fortress behind them. It was spring for the first time in twelve years and it was a truly beautiful place. They met up with Mandor not long afterwards. He was overjoyed to see them. "Where's Fraz?" he asked.

Angel lowered her head. "He never made it," she said regretfully.

"And Jazzaar?"

"He's gone," said Maxus. "Gone for good." He looked up at Angel. "All thanks to Angel."

She smiled slightly.

Maxus knew that she was still tormented about what Jazzaar had said. "Angel, come down from there. We need to talk."

"It's OK, Dad," she reassured, knowing immediately what he was referring to. "You're my father, no matter what anyone says. Nothing will ever change that."

"But still, you have a right to know what happened."

So Angel slid down off Goliath's back and they sat down on the forest floor.

"Before you were born, Jazzaar captured Sonia to get to me…"

"Talk about holding a grudge!" Angel mumbled bitterly.

"And while she was held in the fortress, he—"

"It's OK, Dad, really."

Sonia reached over to hold Angel's hand. "Nine months later, you were born," she smiled, looking over at Jack. "Both of you. We were both so proud; it never occurred to us that Jazzaar could have had any part of it."

"But Mom, none of that matters anyway. We've got you back." Angel's eyes flooded with tears. "I've missed you so much," and they flung their arms around each other.

After fourteen years of lost hugs were caught up on, the family set off back towards the entrance to Equensia, taking Goliath with them.

"Come with us," said Angel to Mandor as they came to the cave.

He shook his head. "That place is too weird for me. Too many monsters!"

Angel smiled. "Well, I'll miss you."

"Maybe you could come back some time?"

"Maybe," she ruffled up the soft fur on his head. "Look after yourself, Mandor, and thank you."

He smiled, which made Angel laugh. She had never seen his teeth before and he looked so cute.

"Thank *you*," he corrected. "Thanks to you, we are free again." He watched the whole family disappear into the rock, knowing that someday they would return. Equensia was that sort of place. Once visited, it would be a part of them forever.

Glossary

Dubring/dub-ring (*noun*) spherical weapon with sharpened gemstones, used for slicing and dismembering

Gragg/grag (*noun*) large carnivorous mammal with long fur and strong scent

Jabbott (flying)/jab-bot (*noun*) small dragon-like creature which develop wings in maturity, often domesticated

Jip/jip (*noun*) carnivorous, long tailed rodent with toxic droppings

Lambin/lam-bin (*noun*) evergreen bush with large, pale leaves used in medicine

Limfit/lim-fit (*noun*) mythological creature once thought to reside in the forests of Equensia

Peapor/pe-a-por (*noun*) fruiting tree with a peeling, pliable bark and a hard wood used frequently for excavation

Skrift/skrift (*noun*) shy, wary creature, with thick camouflaged fur, rarely seen

Willowand/willowand (*noun*) leather strap with magical properties, worn around the waist

Wystrazura/wis-tra-zura (*noun*) resident place for evil

Printed in the United Kingdom
by Lightning Source UK Ltd.
109695UKS00001B/31-48